Let's not fight.

Kate crossed her arms over her chest. "We *told* you, this float is going to be Riverhurst School fifty years ago."

"And *I* told *you* I thought that was a bad idea," Ginger shot back.

"Um, guys, look. Let's not fight about it. . . ." I cut in.

"You're right, Lauren. We shouldn't fight about it — because it's *my* decision what goes on this float," Ginger said firmly.

"What?" Kate cried, hopping down off the float. "It's not your decision! We're the ones who planned the whole thing," she said angrily.

"Well, I think you should at least listen to my idea. After all, it's *my uncle's* float," Ginger retorted. "If I ask him, he'll do whatever I want."

Look for these and other books
in the Sleepover Friends Series:

SLEEPOVER FRIENDS

Kate the Boss

Susan Saunders

AN
APPLE
PAPERBACK

SCHOLASTIC INC.
New York Toronto London Auckland Sydney

ISBN 0-590-43189-7

Copyright © 1990 by Daniel Weiss Associates, Inc. All rights reserved. Published by Scholastic Inc. APPLE PAPERBACKS is a registered trademark of Scholastic Inc.

12 11 10 9 8 7 6 5 4 3 2 1   0 1 2 3 4 5/9

Printed in the U.S.A.   28

First Scholastic printing, October 1990

Kate the Boss

Chapter 1

"As you know, Homecoming is only one week away," Mrs. Mead said. "And next Friday, students will be giving tours of the school all day long. Several people have already signed up to be tour guides, but we still need three more volunteers. Is anyone interested?"

Mrs. Mead is our fifth-grade teacher at Riverhurst Elementary. She was talking about the big celebration the school was having for its fiftieth anniversary — or birthday, I guess you could say. Fifty years ago, Riverhurst Elementary was Riverhurst High School, although personally I find that hard to believe. I can't picture older kids hanging out here because it's so small, and because, well, I feel like it's *our* school.

Anyway, for the Homecoming weekend a whole bunch of people who graduated fifty years ago were coming back to see their old school. There was going to be a big Homecoming parade — complete with floats. And we, the Sleepover Friends, were going to have a float of our very own!

"Come on," Mrs. Mead said. "I only need three more people. Doesn't anyone want to volunteer?"

When no one answered her, she went on: "Let me tell you the names of some other fifth-graders who will be tour guides. Students from 5A to 5C were *eager* to help." Mrs. Mead gave us a meaningful look and picked up a list from her desk. "Let's see . . . Marcy Collins, Jim Dennison, Andrew Gray, Ginger Kinkaid, Christy Soames . . ."

That settled it for me: If Ginger Kinkaid was volunteering, there was no way I wanted to get involved!

Ginger hasn't been living in Riverhurst very long, but already she's one of my least favorite people. By the way, I'm Lauren Hunter. I thought Ginger was great when I first saw her — that was the problem. See, Ginger's uncle — Mr. Blaney — used to be my father's boss at Blaney Realty. So when she came to town, Mr. Blaney and my dad thought it would be a good idea if we became friends.

Wrong! I really liked Ginger at first, but she was only nice to me until she found someone better — Christy Soames, who we nicknamed the Fashion Model. Then Ginger dropped *me* like a hot potato. And while I was friends with Ginger, I practically

2

lost my real best friends because they couldn't stand her. I guess you could say our friendship was an overall disaster. Now Ginger barely even says "hello" to me. I think she's a total snob — and even *that* might be putting it mildly.

I should have known to trust my friends when they didn't like Ginger — especially Kate Beekman. Kate is the most sensible person in the world. She can tell right away if someone's phony. She saw through Ginger the first time she met her. Kate and I have been best friends since we were babies, and we hardly ever disagree. In fact, in all our years together we never had a major difference of opinion about *anything* . . .

. . . until Stephanie Green came along, that is. When Stephanie moved to Riverhurst from the city, I liked her right away. She was funny, she had great ideas, and I loved the way she always dressed in red, black, and white.

Kate and I had been having sleepovers at each other's houses every Friday night since we were in kindergarten. In fact, Kate's dad nicknamed us the Sleepover Twins. I thought Stephanie was great, so I asked her to join us one Friday. What could be better than another Sleepover Friend, right? Wrong! As it turned out, I was just glad both Kate and Stephanie were still talking to *me* by the end of the night! Kate thought Stephanie was an airhead who only

3

cared about rock videos and clothes. She also said Stephanie was too bossy, which was pretty funny because if anyone likes to tell people what to do, it's Kate! As for Stephanie, she thought Kate was way too serious, and bor-r-r-ing!

But I didn't give up. I got Stephanie to invite Kate to a sleepover at her house. After a couple of Mrs. Green's peanut-butter-chocolate-chip cookies, Kate decided sleeping over at Stephanie's wasn't so bad after all. It took a while — and a few more sleep-overs — but little by little they became friends.

It was just in time — because a few months later Patti Jenkins moved to Riverhurst. She and Stephanie had known each other in first grade in the city, so we became friends with her right away. Patti isn't like Stephanie or Kate. She's shy and doesn't really like to be in charge (good thing, too!), but she can do practically anything. She's good at sports, and she's also very smart. Patti's a good friend to have. She'd never let you down, no matter what.

So now the four of us have sleepovers every Friday night. We do practically everything else to-gether, too, especially since we're all in the same class, 5B.

I was in a good mood that day because it was Friday, and we were going to Stephanie's that night. But first we had to get through the last six minutes

4

of school. Mrs. Mead was still waiting for one more person to volunteer. I hoped she wouldn't make us all stay until someone said "yes."

Kate, who sits next to me, passed me a note under her desk.

L — We're definitely not working with you-know-who. Besides, we have to make sure our float is the best in the parade!

—K

I looked at her and nodded in agreement.

"Is that a yes, Lauren?" Mrs. Mead asked me.

Just then the final bell rang. I heaved a huge sigh of relief and jumped up from my seat.

"Think about this over the weekend!" Mrs. Mead called out as everyone scrambled to get their jackets and bolted out the door.

"You weren't seriously going to volunteer, were you, Lauren?" Stephanie asked as we hurried toward the bike rack.

"No way!" I said.

"Yeah, if Ginger and Christy are doing tours, then it's not for us," Kate said. "I mean, we couldn't *possibly* do as good a job as they could," she added sarcastically.

"I wonder how Christy's even going to find her

way around the school," Stephanie said, climbing onto her fifteen-speed.

We all burst out laughing. Christy is kind of an airhead. We call her the Fashion Model because she wears a lot of expensive clothes. I hate to admit it, but she's definitely the best dresser at our school. She looks like a model, too: She's tall and thin, and has long, golden-brown hair. Christy may be an airhead, but she *knows* she's the prettiest girl in the fifth grade.

I got on my bike and we started heading toward my house. My family has just moved, and sometimes I feel like I don't know where I'm going. I keep heading back to our old house on Pine Street. When I'm halfway there I remember that we live on Brio Drive now. Kate and Stephanie both still live on Pine Street. Kate and I had lived next-next door — there was only one house in between us — all our lives. If I wanted to talk to her, I'd just run over. But now I have to call her — *that* feels weird. I guess I'll get used to it eventually, though.

"I can't wait to see the float," Kate said.

"It's only going to be the framework," Patti reminded her.

"I know," Kate replied, "but once I see it I'll be able to imagine how the finished product is going to look."

Blaney Realty, who was sponsoring our float,

was supposed to have delivered the basic framework to my house that morning. I felt kind of responsible for the way the float turned out, since my dad used to work for Mr. Blaney, and they're still good friends. But I knew we'd do a good job, because Kate was in charge of "directing" the float.

Kate wants to be a movie director some day. I think she'll be great at it. She's a real movie fanatic, and she watches them every chance she gets. If Kate had her way, there would be a television station called "All Movies, All the Time"! She's also good at organizing people (bossy!) and being in the video club and watching so many movies, she knows what looks good. So she seemed like a natural choice to be our "float director."

Not that Kate's the only artist in the group — Stephanie is a fantastic artist. Once Kate had come up with her idea for the float, she asked Stephanie to draw some sketches of it so Mr. Blaney could see what she was talking about. Mr. Blaney loved the sketches and the idea.

We were going to show what Riverhurst School looked like fifty years ago. Kate, Patti, and I — plus Henry Larkin and Mark Freedman, some boys in our class — would play students in an old-fashioned classroom. We were going to dress up in old clothes and everything. And Kate had decided that Stephanie would be dressed as the statue in front of the school.

It's called The Spirit of Riverhurst statue, and it looks kind of like the Statue of Liberty.

"Did you find out where we're going to get the stuff to put on the float?" I asked Kate.

"There's an antique furniture store that's going to lend us some desks and a blackboard," Kate said as we pedaled up the hill. "They just want us to put up a little sign that says the stuff comes from their store. We can put it on the side of one of the desks, I guess."

"What do you think we should wear?" Patti asked.

"I'm not sure," Kate said, "but if we go to Clothing Classics, they should be able to give us some ideas. They probably know exactly what was in style back then."

"Do you think anyone wore sneakers?" I asked. I practically live in sneakers.

"No, we'll probably have to wear saddle shoes and bobby socks," Patti said. "Kids used to have to dress up for school, you know — girls had to wear skirts every day."

"I bet no one wore red and black all the time," I teased Stephanie.

"At least you guys get to wear *clothes*," Stephanie groaned, wrinkling her nose. "I have to wear a tablecloth — or is it a curtain?"

"Hey, you should be glad you're not one of

those *naked* statues," I told her. "Like the one in front of the museum."

Stephanie scowled at me. "Can't I just be a student like everyone else?" she begged Kate.

Kate shook her head. "You're the only one whose hair is long enough, like the statue's."

The statue is a woman with long, flowing hair. She's wearing a kind of cape that covers her whole body — and her head — and she's holding a big book and a candle. The plaque underneath the statue says she represents "the joy of learning, the value of education, and the exaltation of humankind everywhere." Or something like that.

"Come on, Stephanie," I said. "Aren't you looking forward to being The Spirit of Riverhurst?"

"Not exactly," she mumbled.

"You should be flattered!" Kate said. "Being a statue is like being put on a pedestal. You're the center of attention, and people stand in front of you and admire you."

Stephanie raised one eyebrow. "I never see anyone admiring that statue. I see a lot of *birds* sitting on it, but that's about all!"

"But it's a landmark," Kate insisted. "It's a very important symbol! Once we get the float all decorated and find our costumes, you'll see what a good idea this is."

While I coasted around the corner onto Brio

Drive, I glanced over at Stephanie. She was frowning. I hoped she wasn't too upset about being a statue. Kate was so excited, I knew she'd be hurt if Stephanie didn't like the idea. Plus, it's bad news when those two disagree about something, because they're both majorly stubborn. I hate getting caught in the middle of one of their arguments.

"I still can't believe you live here," Stephanie said as we turned into the driveway.

"Me, neither!" I admitted. When we first moved, I thought our new house looked like Nightmare Mansion — you know, the one they show before "Friday Night Chillers" on Channel 21. Now I don't think it's that bad, but it still doesn't feel exactly like home.

"Look!" Kate cried. "There's the float!"

Chapter
2

"Wow! Check it out!" Kate laid her bike on the grass and ran up to the garage. Both doors were wide open, and our float was parked inside.

There were two cars in the driveway, my dad's and Mr. Blaney's. I thought I should go in and say "hi," but I couldn't resist taking a look at the float first.

I put my bike in the garage. "It's even bigger than I thought it would be!" I said enthusiastically. So far, our float was only a big piece of wood tacked on to a trailer frame with four wheels — but it still looked good to me.

"I think it's great!" Patti said. "We'll have plenty of room to spread out. And it'll really look like a schoolroom, too."

"Let's see . . ." Kate was walking around the float, looking at it from every angle. "We'll put the desks here . . . maybe in three rows . . . and the blackboard will go right here, of course. Do you think we need any more props?" she asked.

"What else is there?" I replied. "A trash can?"

"Lau-ren!" Kate looked at me like I was crazy. That really was the only other thing I could think of in a classroom, though.

"How about some old schoolbooks?" Stephanie suggested.

"That's a good idea," Kate said, nodding.

"I know — we can make a big wall calendar," Patti said. "To show what year it is."

"I like that idea, too," Kate said. "But what are we going to hang it on? Our classroom isn't going to have walls, remember?"

"We'll think of something," I said.

"Maybe we could find an old globe," Patti said. "You know, one that's on a stand."

"That would look really cool," Kate agreed excitedly. "We could put it right here!" She pointed to the side of the float.

"Kate, where am I going to stand?" Stephanie wanted to know.

"Right up in front. You'll be the first person everyone sees when the float goes past the school," Kate said.

"Oh, great!" Stephanie muttered.

"What's wrong with that?" Kate demanded.

12

"It's going to be so embarrassing!" Stephanie wailed.

"Steph-anie, trust me," Kate said. "Once you're all dressed up, you're going to look fabulous. Imagine how pretty that statue looked when it was first built."

"The woman who posed for it *was* beautiful," Patti put in.

"And that's how you're going to look when you're on the float," Kate insisted. "Beautiful, smart, dedicated, loyal, trustworthy — "

Stephanie held up her hands. "Enough already!"

"Look, I'd volunteer to change places with you, Stephanie, but I don't quite fit the part," I said, holding up a hunk of my hair. My hair is medium length, and as straight as it's possible for hair to be. Stephanie, on the other hand, has long, curly hair with lots of body. She's more the statue type, anyway, because she can be very dramatic. "You'll be great up there — you'll look like a *woman*," I added. "I'd just look like a limp string bean wrapped up in a blanket."

Stephanie giggled. "Okay, okay. I'll do it."

Kate shook her head. "All great directors have to deal with temperamental stars," she said.

"Give me a break," I moaned.

"Actually, there is one thing I *am* worried about," Kate said, hopping up onto the float.

"What's that?" Stephanie asked.

"Well, you really are the only one who can play the statue. What if you get the chicken pox and can't do it? We'll be stuck," Kate said.

A bunch of kids at school had been out with the chicken pox in the past few weeks. Patti, Kate, and I had already had it. Kate and I both got it in the third grade. In fact, we both started going crazy with it the same night, when Kate was sleeping over at my house. When my brother Roger found out, he hung a big sign that said "Quarantine" on my bedroom door and he wouldn't let us come out — until my parents came home! Patti had had the chicken pox when she lived in the city, so she was immune, too.

But the latest epidemic at Riverhurst was pretty serious. One day there were only six people in our class — including the four of us!

"If I was going to get the chicken pox, I would have had it by now," Stephanie said breezily.

"Not necessarily," Patti told her. "You should be careful."

"It's not like I hang around much with anyone else except you guys," Stephanie said.

"Still, you could get it from anyone in our class," Kate reminded her. "Or anyone else at school. But I asked my father, and he thinks you probably have a natural immunity to it." Kate's father is a doctor, so she knows more than we do about this stuff.

"See? What did I tell you?" Stephanie grinned.

"Just don't kiss anybody, and you'll be fine," Kate said seriously.

"Kate!" we all screamed. None of us has kissed a boy yet — and we're not about to! Kate takes things so seriously sometimes, it's funny.

"What's going on in here?" my father asked. He and Mr. Blaney walked into the garage.

"Hi, Dad. Hi, Mr. Blaney. We were just admiring the float," I replied.

"That's funny, I thought you were yelling at Kate," my father joked.

"We were just telling her what a good idea the float was," Patti said. She has the most innocent face of all of us, so she gets us out of sticky situations a lot of the time.

"Hello, Lauren. How are you?" Mr. Blaney asked me. He's a really nice guy. You'd never know he was related to Ginger Kinkaid, except that they both have reddish-brown hair. Mr. Blaney is tall, but he's not thin — actually, his body is sort of pear-shaped.

"I'm fine," I said.

"None of you have the chicken pox, do you? I heard it's going around school like gangbusters," Mr. Blaney said.

I bit my lip and tried not to giggle. Where did my parents' friends get words like "gangbusters," anyway? It reminded me of my grandfather, who's always calling Roger a "teenybopper." Were we going to have to say silly things like that when we were pretending to be students from fifty years ago?

"Well, actually, we were just talking about that," Kate said. "We've all had it before — except Stephanie."

"Take care of yourself, then," Mr. Blaney advised Stephanie. "So what do you think, girls?" he went on, pointing at the float. "Is it good enough to put Blaney Realty's name on it?"

"Definitely!" I said. "Wait until we get the props on it — it's going to look dynamite!"

"We'll do a very professional job for you," Kate told Mr. Blaney. "You can trust us."

My father looked at me and raised one eyebrow. He knows Kate pretty well, and I could tell he thought it was funny — and typical — how she had totally taken over the project.

"I think it's a fantastic idea. I'm already impressed. The drawings you did were excellent, Stephanie," Mr. Blaney said. He strolled around the float.

"We're going to put the desks here, so we're facing forward," Kate demonstrated from on top of the float. "The blackboard will go here, and we're going to get some old schoolbooks and a globe, and maybe a calendar."

"I can't wait to see the finished result!" Mr. Blaney said. "I think we're going to have one of the

16

best floats in the parade — if not *the* best. I know Ginger can't wait to ride on it."

I practically fell over. Ginger Kinkaid on our float?! He had to be joking!

I glanced at Kate. She had a stunned expression on her face, too. Stephanie was staring at her black ankle boots. Her hair hid her face, but I was sure she was scowling at the garage floor.

"Oh, will Ginger be riding with us?" Patti finally said — very politely, I might add. I was glad she was around. If she hadn't been, I probably would have just stood there with my mouth hanging open until dinnertime.

"Yes, didn't she tell you?" Mr. Blaney asked us. "We spoke about it a few days ago when she was over at my house for dinner."

"No-o-o-o," I stammered, trying not to sound too put out. "She didn't say a word."

"We *are* in separate classes," Patti added with a smile. "She probably just didn't get a chance yet."

"I'm sure that's what happened," my father said, looking at me. He knew how I felt about Ginger after our so-called friendship, and he was probably afraid I was going to say something about her in front of Mr. Blaney.

"You know her friend Christy, don't you?" Mr. Blaney asked.

We all nodded slowly. Boy, did we ever!

"I think she's going to ride on the float, too," he informed us. "They both loved your idea when I told them about it, Kate. And when I gave it some thought, I realized the exhibit on the float might look better if the class was a little larger. Don't you agree?"

"Well, if we can all fit . . . sure," Kate mumbled.

"The more, the merrier, that's what I always say!" Mr. Blaney said happily.

I looked at Kate. Not when the "more" was Ginger!

Chapter 3

"It's a disaster," I said, tossing my sleeping bag onto the floor.

"Seriously!" Kate added. She was lying on one of the fold-out couches in Stephanie's apartment. It's not an apartment, really — it's more like a playhouse. Just before Stephanie's twin brother and sister were born, her parents built a small house in their backyard for Stephanie to use when we have sleepovers.

It's one big room, and it's all decorated in red, black, and white, natch. There's a TV, a phone, two fold-out sleeper sofas, and even a small refrigerator. We love having sleepovers at Stephanie's because we don't have to deal with little sisters, older brothers — or parents!

"But what are we going to do?" Patti asked anxiously.

"I'm glad you're finally here, Lauren, so we can figure it out," Stephanie sighed. "Have a seat."

I collapsed onto the sofa next to her. "Maybe this is just a bad dream. Mr. Blaney didn't *really* say that Ginger and Christy wanted to ride on our float, did he?"

Stephanie, Patti, and Kate all nodded glumly.

"Oh," I said. So much for *that* theory.

"Ginger's going to turn our float into a nightmare," Kate predicted. "Just imagine having to work with her all next week after school!"

Stephanie giggled.

"I don't see what's so funny about that," I said.

"I was just thinking — Christy probably won't even remember what day the parade is," Stephanie sputtered. "She'll be so worried about how she looks, she'll end up riding on someone else's float!"

"That would be great — if only she'd take Ginger with her," Kate groaned. "Maybe we could tell them to meet us before the parade. Then we can meet someplace else and they'll miss the whole thing!"

"Kate! We can't do that!" I cried. "Mr. Blaney knows they're supposed to be on the float, and it's *his* float."

"And she's his *niece*," Patti added.

"Right." I tapped my fingers on the arm of the

sofa. "But maybe we could do something that isn't so obvious."

"Like what?" Stephanie asked eagerly. She's always interested in a good scheme.

I shrugged. "I don't know. Hey, do you have any snacks around?" I don't think well on an empty stomach. Even though I had just eaten dinner an hour before, I was already hungry again. I have an incredible appetite and everyone always makes fun of me for it. Kate calls me the Endless Stomach and the Bottomless Pit. But I can't help it. Besides, I go running with my brother four or five times a week, so even if I do eat more than any of my friends I get more exercise than they do, too. It evens out — at least I hope so!

"Sure. I don't know about you guys, but I feel like eating whenever I'm bummed," Stephanie said. She stood up and walked over to the refrigerator. "I don't care if I look like a blimp, either."

I can eat as much as I want and never gain weight, but Stephanie isn't as lucky. She says her face gets all puffy when she pigs out, although I've never noticed it.

"I definitely feel like eating whenever I'm down," I said. I got up and started getting plates and cups out of the cupboard.

"Oh, yeah? When *don't* you?" Kate teased me.

Stephanie handed me a tin of her mom's special peanut-butter-chocolate-chip cookies. "This is just for starters," she said. Then she took a six-pack of Dr Pepper, a bowl of dip, a box of cold fried chicken, and a jar of pickles out of the refrigerator.

I opened the cabinet beneath the counter and grabbed a big bag of ranch-flavored potato chips. We were in for some serious munchies!

"I have an idea," Patti said. "Why don't we check our horoscope and see what it says for next week?"

"Oh, pull-eze," Kate groaned. "Not that mumbo-jumbo again." She doesn't believe in horoscopes, fortune-tellers, or anything like that.

"It's worth a shot," Stephanie agreed, setting the food down on the coffee table in front of Kate and Patti. "I just bought next month's *Teen Topics* — it's right over there." *Teen Topics* — or TT for short — is our absolute favorite magazine.

Patti picked the magazine off the counter and flipped through it while I ripped open the bag of chips. "So what does it say?" I asked, dragging a chip through the dip. "Are we doomed?"

"When is Ginger's birthday?" Patti wanted to know.

"May, I think," I said.

"Ah-hah! She's a Taurus," Stephanie exclaimed. "The bull — that figures!"

22

"Lauren, listen to your horoscope!" Patti said. " 'This is a good month for getting things done, but beware of a Taurus who may try to stand in your way,' " she read. "They must mean Ginger!"

"Isn't your brother's birthday in May, too?" Kate put in. She's very suspicious when it comes to predictions.

"Sure, but they're obviously not talking about him," I said with a wave of my hand. "Does it say what I should do?"

Patti shook her head. She skimmed the rest of the "It's Written in the Stars" column. "Hey, Stephanie, yours says something really exciting is going to happen to you this month!"

Stephanie grinned. "That's good, as long as it's not the chicken pox."

Kate sighed loudly. "I think I'll see what's on TV," she said, picking up the remote and flicking it on.

"Maybe we could call one of the radio talk shows and ask them for advice," Stephanie said. She picked up her second cookie and started chewing on it.

"I don't think so," I said. "They'd probably laugh at us. Besides, Ginger might be listening and she'd recognize our voices."

"Yeah," Stephanie agreed, stuffing another cookie into her mouth. This was serious — I had never seen her eat so much! I wondered if something else was bothering her, like maybe her part on the float. . . .

Meanwhile, Kate flipped through every channel on the TV, stopping for about two seconds at each one. "This really is a bad dream," she said, abruptly turning it off. "It's Friday night and there aren't even any good movies on!" She reached into the bag and took out a handful of potato chips. I had a feeling that if we didn't think of a solution to the Ginger problem fast, we were *all* going to turn into blimps!

"All right, you guys, how are we going to get Ginger off our float?" I said, taking charge for once. "We have to come up with something *tonight*. Otherwise we're not going to be able to fall asleep and we're going to have a horrible weekend."

"Well, maybe if we make the float look really bad, she and Christy won't want to be on it," Patti said. "I mean, you know how those two are into their looks and everything."

"We can't do that," Kate objected. "It's a great idea and we've already spent lots of time on it. *We* don't want to look bad. Besides, Mr. Blaney likes the float, too."

"What if we *accidentally* wreck the float?" Stephanie suggested. Stephanie's famous for her wild ideas.

"Are you out of your mind?!" Kate cried.

"Okay, okay. I know! We can get Wayne Miller to be one of the students on the float," Stephanie said. Wayne Miller is the grossest boy in our school. His idea of fun is pulling wings off flies. I think he also holds the school record for the longest and loudest burp.

"Yeah! We could tell Ginger that she has to share a desk with Wayne if she wants to be on the float," I added.

"She'd be gone in two seconds!" Stephanie said gleefully. "She wouldn't be caught dead sitting next to him!"

"Aren't you forgetting something? *We'd* have to be on the float with Wayne, too," Kate declared.

I wrinkled my nose. Parading down the middle of Riverhurst next to Wayne Miller was the last thing I wanted to do. It sounded even worse than riding with Ginger Kinkaid. The worst part was that Wayne's cousin, Bitsy Barton, who's a friend of ours, told me that Wayne sort of *likes* me. Can you imagine anything more embarrassing than the most obnoxious boy in school having a crush on you?! Wayne Miller was definitely out! "If Wayne rides with us, we'll probably be teased by everyone at school for years afterward!" I said.

"Okay, so maybe that wasn't the greatest idea in the world," Stephanie said, taking a sip of Dr Pepper. "But we have to do *something*!"

"Maybe the clothes store won't have enough costumes for everybody," Patti said.

Kate shook her head. "They have *tons* of old clothes. Face it — we're stuck with Ginger. And Christy."

"Oh, no, I just thought of something else," I said. "You know how Ginger thinks she's so good at art. What if she decides she wants to change the float around? I mean, she told Mr. Blaney she loved our idea, but she's not exactly the type to sit back and watch."

"No kidding!" Kate said. "She's really bossy."

I quickly ate a chip so I wouldn't snicker. Look who's talking!

"She'll definitely want to be front and center," Patti agreed.

"Maybe she'll want to be The Spirit of Riverhurst Elementary," Stephanie murmured. She sounded almost hopeful.

"No. She probably thinks it's going to be one of those floats with princesses on it, who wear furs and hold flowers and wave to the crowd." I stood up and walked around the room, wiggling my hips, doing a little fake wave, and smiling from ear to ear.

Stephanie and Patti both started laughing, but Kate still looked upset. "Lauren, I think you've been eating too much sugar!" she said.

26

"I can see it now," Stephanie gasped. "Home-coming Queen, Ginger Kinkaid!"

"Come on, you guys, this isn't funny," Kate insisted.

I sat back down and grabbed the last cookie.

"I think we should just tell her what the float is going to be and what her part is," Kate said firmly. "You know, tell her it's already been approved by Mr. Blaney and we can't change it around now."

"That sounds like the best idea," Patti agreed. "We won't see her until Monday at school, right? What if we get as much of the float done over the weekend as we can?"

Kate nodded eagerly. "Yeah! That way she won't be able to make any changes — it'll be all set. Do you think that'll be okay with your parents?" she asked me.

"I don't see why not," I replied.

"Good. Everything will work out fine," Kate said.

I wasn't so sure, but I decided to keep my doubts to myself.

"Now that we know how we're going to deal with Ginger, do you think we could actually have some fun tonight?" Stephanie asked with a pointed look at Kate.

"Have you ever thought about how many funny

nicknames we could give Ginger?" I said. "Ginger Ale, Ginger Bread — "

"Ginger Snap!" Kate added with a giggle.

"Her real name isn't even Ginger, it's Virginia," Patti said.

"Look, let's forget about her already," Stephanie suggested. "We have better things to do than talk about Ginger Kinkaid. How about a little game of Truth or Dare?" she added, with a wicked grin.

I should have known — we all love that game. Actually, I don't always love it, because sometimes you have to admit things that are incredibly embarrassing — things you wouldn't even want to tell your best friends. But it's also kind of cool because we find out everything about each other, and I think that makes us better friends.

"Okay, who's first?" Kate said, moving closer.

"Let's see . . . I'll pick Patti." Stephanie looked at her and raised her eyebrows. "Truth or dare, my dear?"

Patti didn't answer right away. It was hard to know what to do — Stephanie usually gives out really hard dares.

"Truth," she finally said, biting her lip.

"What's the stupidest thing you've ever said to a boy?" Stephanie demanded.

Patti's face turned red. "Do I really have to tell you?"

Stephanie threw a potato chip at her. "You know the rules!"

"All right, all right! Well, once I was, uh, walking through the gym, on my way to the art studio. And a bunch of sixth-graders were playing basketball. One of them saw me and I heard him say, 'Hey, she'd be great on our team!' As if that wasn't embarrassing enough," Patti said, rolling her eyes. She's the tallest girl in our class — even taller than me — and she's taller than most of the boys, too. "Then this one obnoxious boy said, 'Forget it. She may be tall, but girls can't play with boys. They're too klutzy.' That made me mad and I said — " Patti started giggling " — I may be a *boy*, but I can play ball any day!' They all burst out laughing." Patti shook her head. "It was totally humiliating — 'I may be a *boy*.' Ugh! How stupid can you get?"

We all started laughing. "What boys were playing?" Stephanie wanted to know.

"You didn't ask me that," Patti said. "I don't have to tell you."

"Oh, come on," Kate urged.

"Forget it," Patti insisted. "It's my turn now. Stephanie, truth or dare?"

"Mmm . . . truth."

"Who do you have a crush on this week?" Patti asked. That was a good question — Stephanie is always changing her mind about who she likes.

29

"This might take her a few minutes," I joked.

Stephanie bit her lip. "Promise you won't get mad, Kate?" she asked.

Kate looked confused. "Why should I get mad?"

"Because you like the same person I like," Stephanie admitted.

"Is he a rock star?" Patti asked.

"We're not playing twenty questions!" I reminded them. "Come on, Stephanie. Who is it?"

"Taylor Sprouse," Stephanie finally mumbled.

"You've got to be kidding!" I said. "What is this? Some kind of contagious disease?" Taylor was the *last* person I expected Stephanie to like. Of course, I had been pretty surprised when I'd found out Kate had a crush on him — even if Kate *said* she'd gotten over it. Taylor's in the sixth grade, and his most noticeable characteristic is that he dresses all in black. I think he's trying for the rock-star look, because he plays the guitar — only he'll need about two thousand more lessons before he's any good. He's also in the Video Club, and the way he carries on you'd think he invented creative filmmaking. I mean, the guy acts like he's the coolest thing around.

"You'd both better give up on him," I said. "The only person Taylor Sprouse is interested in is himself." It's true. He makes a point of checking himself out every chance he gets. I've even seen him combing his hair, using the reflection off the windows in the lunch room! Talk about conceited! He *is* pretty cute, but boy does he ever know it!

"I don't even like him anymore," Kate squawked. "I only like his videos. He's too stuck up."

"I'm not so sure about that," Stephanie said.

"Oh? Do you know something we don't?" I asked.

Stephanie shrugged. "I talked to him last week and he was kind of nice to me."

"So that's why you have a crush on him!" Patti said.

"That's not the only reason," Stephanie argued. "I think he's cute."

Kate didn't say anything. She *said* she didn't like him anymore, but I wondered if secretly she still did. None of us had ever liked the same boy before — unless you can count Kevin DeSpain, our favorite movie star, or Russell Carter, the lead singer of the Boodles.

"Kate, you really don't like him anymore, right? You don't care that I like him, do you?" Stephanie asked.

Kate didn't answer.

"Kate?" Stephanie said more loudly.

"Oh — sorry," she said. "I was just thinking . . ." she said slowly. "Maybe we should get up really early tomorrow. You know? To work on the float. Do you have an alarm clock out here, Stephanie?"

"I think so," Stephanie said. "Okay, Lauren, it's your turn."

Before I could say I was willing to take the dare, Kate interrupted. "Do you think we could set it now?"

"What's the big hurry?" Stephanie asked. She leaned over and picked up the clock on the night table beside the couch.

"I just don't want us to forget and oversleep," Kate replied.

Stephanie sighed loudly. "What time should I set it for? Nine?"

"Set it for eleven," I chimed in. I hate getting up early. After all, the whole point of weekends is to sleep late, isn't it?

But Kate shook her head. "Seven o'clock," she said.

"Ka-ate!" we all shrieked.

"We have to get over to Lauren's and start working on the float," Kate said firmly.

"How about eight-thirty?" Stephanie groaned, pressing the buttons on the clock.

"Seven," Kate insisted.

I was used to Kate being a little bossy, but this was too much. We always sleep late on Saturdays after our sleepovers — because we always stay up really late! Besides, I don't even get up at seven on school days!

"Then I guess we should go to sleep now," Patti said, unzipping her duffel bag and taking out her nightshirt.

"Definitely." Kate got up and went into the bathroom to brush her teeth.

"I feel like we're in the army or something," Stephanie whispered to Patti and me once Kate had closed the door.

"Sergeant Beekman in command," I nodded.

"Look at it this way," Patti murmured. "We'll have the best float in the parade."

"Yeah, and it'll be finished tomorrow by noon!" I said.

Chapter 4

We ate breakfast quickly the next morning, then got on our bikes and headed straight for my house. I was feeling pretty zonked because we'd hardly gotten any sleep. Even though we had tried to go to bed early, we kept thinking of more things to talk about. It was after two when we said good-night for the last time. And thanks to Kate, the alarm went off promptly at seven o'clock.

The second we got to my house, Kate jumped off her bike. "Okay, let's get going," she said in a brisk voice.

Stephanie yawned loudly. "What should we do first?"

"Let's make a list of everything we need to decorate the float," Kate said.

Kate's always making lists — she's incredibly organized. Even her bedroom is neat. Mine, on the other hand, is more like a natural disaster area.

"Lauren, could you get us a notebook or something?" she asked.

I nodded. When I walked into the house I heard my parents talking in the kitchen. "Hi!" I called out. "It's me!" My kitten, Rocky, ran out to meet me. I leaned over to pet him. "Hi, did you miss me?" I asked. He meowed, so I took that for a "yes."

"Me who?" my father called back.

"Very funny," I said, entering the kitchen.

My mother looked up from the newspaper. "What are you doing home so early?" she asked.

"We wanted to start working on the float," I told them. I grabbed a notepad and pen off the counter. "Can we borrow these?"

My mother shrugged. "Sure."

"Thanks!" I dashed back outside. Patti and Stephanie were sitting on the float in the garage. They looked pretty tired. Kate was pacing back and forth on top of the float.

She frowned when I gave her the notepad. "Couldn't you find something a little bigger?" she asked. I shrugged. Was Kate going to act like this all week?

"Props," Kate began, writing it down. "Desks, chairs, globe . . ."

"Some old schoolbooks," Patti added. "And a calendar, if we can make one that stands up."

"Good." Kate tapped the pen against the pad. "Anything else?" She was sounding more like Sergeant Beekman every minute.

"How about a bookcase, or one of those big stands that you put a dictionary on?" I suggested.

Kate jotted it down. "Mmmm. That should do it. If we think of anything else we can always add it later. Now, on to clothes." She flipped to the next page.

"Old sweaters, skirts, and shoes from Clothing Classics," Patti said in a bored voice.

"And a curtain for me," Stephanie added. She looked at me and made a face.

"No, I think a sheet would work better," Kate said thoughtfully. "One green sheet," she murmured, writing it down. "What size do you think — single or double?"

Stephanie groaned. "This is ridiculous!"

"What is?" a voice called from the doorway of the garage.

I couldn't believe my ears. We weren't the only ones who had gotten up at the crack of dawn!

Kate dropped her pen, which clattered against the wooden float. "Ginger! What are you doing here?" she demanded.

"I came to help get the float ready, what else?" Ginger replied. She strolled into the garage with Christy Soames right behind her. Ginger had on jeans and an oversized sweater that had swirls of green, blue, and gold all over it.

"Me, too," Christy announced, striding into the garage. She was wearing a sweater just like Ginger's, only it was pink, purple, and electric blue. She had a tiny pocketbook slung over one shoulder. She's the only girl in the fifth grade with a pocketbook — the rest of us just lug our stuff around in knapsacks and book bags. To tell you the truth, Christy's the only one who could pull off carrying one without looking stupid.

"So where *is* the float?" Christy asked, looking around.

I laughed. "You're looking at it," I told her.

"That thing?" Christy wrinkled her nose.

"Obviously, we have a lot of work to do," Ginger declared. She walked over and examined the float more closely. "It's a bit, uh . . . old-fashioned, but it'll do." Suddenly she sounded as if *she* were the one in charge of the float.

"It's supposed to look old-fashioned," Kate told her. "That's the whole point."

"What do you mean?" Ginger asked.

"Well, we're showing the school the way it was fifty years ago, right? So it shouldn't look like a modern school," Kate explained. "I'm sure Mr. Blaney told you about our plan. We're going to use old furniture and dress up in old clothes and everything."

Ginger started walking around the float. "Oh, yeah . . . my uncle did say something about that," she said. "But I don't think it's such a good idea."

Kate put her hands on her hips. "Oh, and I suppose you have a better one?" she asked.

"As a matter of fact, I do," Ginger said. "I mean, I'm not sure exactly what we should do, but I think it should be more modern — you know, something a little more up to date."

"But the whole point of the Homecoming is to celebrate the history of Riverhurst School," Patti pointed out.

"And your uncle already agreed on our idea for the float," I added.

"So? I'm sure that when I tell him my idea, he'll agree that it's much better," Ginger said, flipping her long reddish-brown hair over her shoulder. Ginger was always bragging that her uncle would do *anything* for her.

Stephanie glared at her. "Okay, let's hear it."

"You guys are going to *love* it," Christy predicted.

Somehow I doubted that. I glanced up at Kate. She was really mad, I could tell. One of her eyebrows was raised and she was looking at Ginger as if she were an alien from another planet.

"Well, instead of wearing a bunch of old clothes, why don't we wear new stuff?" Ginger said.

"You know, the hot looks of the moment." Kate snorted, but Ginger paid no attention. "We could just be ourselves — today's students," she went on. "Or maybe we could pretend to be students of the future. You know, put a couple of computers on the float and dress in really wild colors like neon and stuff." She paused for a breath. "So what do you think?"

"I think it'll look dynamite," Christy said. I wasn't surprised. She would agree to anything with high fashion in it. She and Ginger were made for each other.

But I knew from personal experience how pushy Ginger could be. When I was friends with her she wanted us to buy the same sweater, style our hair the same way . . . you name it.

Kate was still pacing around on top of the float. "It wouldn't work," she said.

"Why not?" Ginger wanted to know.

"Because," Kate said, "we don't even know what schools will look like in the future. This isn't supposed to be a science fiction float. We're doing a *real* portrayal of life at Riverhurst School fifty years ago!"

"But that's soooo boring," Christy groaned. "This would be something totally new and different."

"That's for sure," Stephanie murmured. Even though she didn't say anything else, I could tell she

39

was kind of interested in Ginger's idea. Actually, even I didn't think it was so terrible. The idea of wearing new clothes — like jeans and sneakers — sounded a lot more fun to me than dressing up in an old skirt and pearls!

"We could call it 'Students of Tomorrow,' " Ginger suggested. "Or maybe 'The New Wave of Students.' "

"That sounds like we're surfing," Kate complained.

"Well, whatever." Ginger threw up her hands. "You can't expect me to think of everything."

"Obviously," Kate muttered, jumping down from the float and walking over to me. "The nerve!" she hissed, making a horrible face.

"Calm down," I whispered back. I didn't want Kate to blow up at Ginger — after all, she *was* Mr. Blaney's niece. What if she told him we were mean to her? He might change his mind about sponsoring the float. Besides, if Ginger really was going to be on the float with us, we had to work things out somehow. But I had a feeling it wasn't going to be easy.

"Can we have a few minutes to talk this over?" Patti asked.

"No problem," Ginger said, with a shrug. "Christy, come over here and stand on the float. I want to see how different poses look."

Christy sauntered over to Ginger, and the rest of us gathered in a tight huddle.

"I can't believe this!" Kate exploded.

"It's just like we thought," Patti admitted.

"She's taking over the whole thing," Stephanie agreed.

"What do you think we should do?" I asked them.

Kate shook her head. "If we use *her* idea, we'll end up embarrassing ourselves in front of the whole town!" she said. "We've got to just stick with our original plan. I mean, Mr. Blaney approved the idea and it's his opinion that counts, not hers. Besides, we've already put a lot of work into this idea. We can't scrap it now."

We all nodded in agreement.

"It's four against two," Kate continued. "So what we say, *goes*."

"Hey, Stephanie," Ginger called. "Didn't you do some drawings for the float?"

"Y-Yes," Stephanie answered slowly.

"Can I see them?" Ginger asked.

Stephanie walked over to the corner of the garage and took the drawings off the shelf where we had stored them. "Why do you want these?" she said as she handed them to Ginger.

Ginger shrugged. "Oh, I just want to make a few adjustments."

"What do you mean?" Stephanie asked suspiciously.

"So we can set up the float the new way," Ginger explained. She skimmed the drawings. "Like the first thing we have to do is get rid of those desks. We could put TVs on the float instead."

"TVs?" Kate repeated.

"Everyone says that in the future kids won't go to school — they'll stay home and learn from video teachers instead," Christy announced.

I stared at her. Maybe she wasn't such an airhead after all. She certainly seemed to know what she was talking about.

"Exactly. Okay, so we've got the TVs here," Ginger said, pointing. "Then we'll put a computer or two over here. My dad can probably borrow some from work." Ginger's father works at Blaney Realty. He's in charge of their computer system. "And, presto, the look of the future."

"What about costumes?" Christy asked.

"We should look kind of space age," Ginger said. "You know — wear really bright clothes in like silver and gold and neon so we'll really stand out." She held out the drawing to Stephanie. "What's this up here?"

"Oh, that . . ." Stephanie mumbled. "It's, uhh . . . The Spirit of Riverhurst."

"Not that grody statue!" Christy exclaimed. "Like what a bummer!"

Stephanie nodded slowly.

"We have to get rid of that, too," Ginger said. "That is just way too old-fashioned."

A smile crept across Stephanie's face. She definitely did not want to be that statue!

"Maybe we could replace the statue with a big tape player and play some rock music," Christy said. "Then we could dance on top of the float!"

"You guys, this isn't supposed to be a rock video!" Kate argued.

Christy rolled her eyes. "It's just an idea," she said.

"We're going to have to work out all the details," Ginger declared. "But now that I've seen the basic framework, I think I can take it from there."

Kate looked like one of those cartoon characters with the smoke coming out of its ears. She was going to explode any minute! I decided to rush Ginger's departure so that she and Kate wouldn't get into a gigantic fight.

"Wow! Look at the time!" I said, pointing to my watch. "We have to get going, Kate." We had told the clerk at Clothing Classics that we'd be in that morning.

"You're right. We have a *very* important appointment," Kate said, glaring at Ginger.

"Oh, yeah — so do we," Ginger said, "at the mall." Christy giggled. "We're going shopping," Ginger added — as if the two of them ever did anything else! "Come on, Christy, let's go." She and Christy walked out of the garage. "See you later!" Ginger called over her shoulder. "Keep thinking of good ideas for our float!"

"Yeah, we'll think about it," I called after her. If I knew Kate, we wouldn't be thinking of anything *but* the float!

"Bye!" Christy drawled, as she and Ginger started heading up the sidewalk.

"And good riddance!" Kate muttered.

Chapter 5

"She wants to take over the whole thing!" Kate fumed once Ginger and Christy were out of earshot. "She didn't even try to suggest a compromise!"

"Do you think she'll tell Mr. Blaney about her plans for the float?" Patti asked.

I shrugged. "She might." That's what was worrying me, too. If Ginger told her uncle that Kate was against her idea, he might just turn the float over to her and leave us completely out of it! I couldn't see Mr. Blaney going for neon clothes, TVs, and booming rock music, though. After all, the name of his company was going to be in big letters on the side of the float. Still, Ginger was his favorite niece.

"Even if she does, he's already given us the go-ahead," Kate said angrily. "He knows how much work we've put into this. I still say we should try and finish as much as we can this weekend."

"What if Ginger shows up again?" Stephanie asked.

"We'll tell her that we're going along with the original plan," Kate insisted. "If she doesn't like it, we'll just have to cut the float in half."

Patti and I exchanged nervous glances. Kate sounded awfully determined and when she gets like that, she won't let anything — or anybody — stand in her way.

Kate grabbed the notepad off the top of the float. "Now, come on, gang! Let's hit Clothing Classics!"

Stephanie pulled a big floppy hat over her head. "So what do you think?" she said, posing in front of the mirror.

"You look abzolootlee beauteefool, dahling," I said in my best French accent (not that I know a word of French, but I've picked up a lot from watching movies with Kate). I slipped a beret on my head. "How about this?"

Stephanie giggled. "Pretty ugly, actually."

"Thanks a lot!" I said, pretending to be hurt.

"Ooh, look at that!" Stephanie ran over to one of the clothes racks and took down a red short-sleeved blouse with black trim around the collar and sleeves. "I *have* to get this," she said dramatically.

"Steph-anie," I said, laughing. "I don't think that's exactly what you're looking for. . . ."

46

She turned it around. *Abe's Towing Service* was embroidered in big black letters on the back. "I guess it isn't so wonderful after all," Stephanie admitted.

She and I were checking out all the fun stuff at Clothing Classics, while Patti and Kate were picking up the things we needed for the parade. The sales clerk was showing them the outfits she had selected for us.

I usually don't like antique clothes, but Clothing Classics is great. I had already picked out an old silver pin I wanted to get to put on my jean jacket. Stephanie was looking for something to go with her black jeans — or, should I say, her newest pair of black jeans. She has about a dozen pairs, at least! If Christy's the best-dressed girl at our school, then Stephanie's definitely a close second, if you ask me.

"Hey, Lauren!" Stephanie said excitedly. "Come over here." She held up a red blouse with black polka dots. It looked totally fifties.

"That's cool," I told her. "How much is it?"

Stephanie hunted for the price tag. "Too much," she said with a frown.

"Maybe you could find something like it at the mall," I suggested. "It might be cheaper if it's brand new. That sounds weird, doesn't it?"

Stephanie smiled. "Yeah. You're right. Let's go to the mall after this, okay?"

"For sure." Ginger and Christy aren't the only

fifth-graders around who love to shop!

"Hey, Lauren, can I ask you something?" Stephanie said, putting the blouse back on the rack. "What did you think of Ginger's idea?"

I shrugged. "I don't know. I guess she has a point about our idea being too old-fashioned. I wouldn't mind wearing regular clothes, you know?"

Stephanie nodded vigorously. "That's just the way I feel. I mean, Kate's idea is great . . . but if I have to wear a sheet in front of the whole town I'm going to die. I'm not saying we should go along with Ginger's idea or let her be director or anything. But maybe we could use some of her suggestions, like making the float more up-to-date."

"But you know Kate," I said. "She doesn't like to change her plans for anyone, especially not for someone she hates."

"Yeah, and it would be pretty awful having Ginger telling us what to do," Stephanie admitted. "I guess we're stuck with the historical look."

"And you're stuck with the toga," I said with a sympathetic smile.

"Lauren! Stephanie! Get over here!" Kate called from the back of the store.

Stephanie and I walked over and found Kate and Patti standing outside the dressing rooms. Patti was holding a giant armful of clothes. She looked pretty worn out. "Look how many clothes they're going to

lend us! We're going to have totally cool outfits!"
Kate said confidently.

I glanced at the stuff Patti was holding. I couldn't
exactly say that any of it looked totally cool — at
least not by today's standards. Maybe it was cool fifty
years ago, but the only people who were going to
know that were our grandparents!

"Now, I just want to figure out who should wear
what," Kate went on. She picked a yellow blouse
out of the heap of clothes. "Lauren, I think this has
your name on it." She held it out to me.

I grimaced. "Do I *have* to try it on?" I said.

Kate shook her head. "No, just hold it up against
you so I can see how it looks."

I took a deep breath. If there's one thing I hate,
it's yellow. I draped the blouse over myself and
glanced in the mirror. "I can't wear this!" I burst out.

"It's perfect!" Kate said at the same time.

"What do you mean, it's perfect? This shade of
yellow makes me look as if I just got out of the
hospital."

Mrs. Munson, the woman who was helping us,
came up behind me. "How nice!" she said. "With
a plaid skirt, you'll have a real vintage look."

I wasn't sure I wanted one. I'd rather be The
Spirit of Riverhurst statue, I thought to myself. At least
then I'd have an excuse for looking dumb!

"See?" Kate said proudly. "You want the float

to be accurate, don't you? Now, let's see . . . Patti, why don't you try on this?'' She pulled out a bubble-gum pink sweater that had a huge rose embroidered on the front of it.

Patti gave it a doubtful look. Pink isn't exactly her best color. But she handed the other clothes to Kate, and slowly held the sweater up in front of her. ''Uh, I don't think so,'' she said. ''Flowers aren't really my thing.''

''It is pretty geeky,'' Stephanie added.

''Girls, girls! What seems geeky to you now was simply all the rage fifty years ago,'' Mrs. Munson put in. ''Trust me!''

I couldn't imagine a sweater like that *ever* being in fashion — it was hideous. Kate's idea was losing its charm. I had thought our clothes were at least going to be flattering — instead, we were dressing up like my great aunt Helene, and even my mother says her clothes were *never* in style!

It's not that Kate's a bad dresser. She was just getting so caught up in making the float the most authentic one in the history of parades that all she cared about was getting the look exactly.

Kate tapped her finger against her chin. ''You know, I'm sure I saw a sweater just like that in an old forties movie once,'' she said with a gleam in her eye. ''We'll take it!''

''But Kate, I — '' Patti began.

"I'm going to wear a plain dark skirt with a blazer," Kate continued, ignoring Patti. She checked off a few things on her list. "We're all set, except for shoes."

I didn't even want to imagine what the shoes were going to look like! "Do I have to wear yellow shoes, too?" I asked.

"I'm not sure yet," Kate said. She didn't even notice that I was joking!

"I'll have all these clothes cleaned for you by Tuesday," Mrs. Munson said. "We can do any alterations then, too."

"Why don't we pick out the shoes then?" Patti suggested.

"Yeah. I've had enough, uh, antique shopping," I said.

"What about the clothes for Henry and Mark?" Stephanie asked.

"We already picked those out. Their stuff is fairly basic. You know, pants and jackets," Kate said. "They don't get to wear anything interesting like we do."

Lucky them! I thought. Maybe I could convince Kate that we needed another boy on the float to take *my* place. . . .

"They'll have to come in with you on Tuesday, okay, girls?" Mrs. Munson said. "And we'll make sure we have the right sizes for them."

"Henry and Mark are going to love that," Patti said with a grin.

"They'll get over it," Kate said.

"What about Christy and Ginger?" Patti asked. "Shouldn't we pick out clothes for them, too?"

Kate shook her head. "They can worry about their own clothes. Besides, they might not even be on the float. So, what do you guys want to do now? Should we go back to Lauren's and — "

"Guard the float?" I interrupted.

Kate actually smiled. I was surprised. I was beginning to think she'd completely lost her sense of humor. "Work on the float is what I was going to say," she finished.

"Lauren and I want to go to the mall," Stephanie said. "I need to find a shirt."

"And I need to eat lunch," I added. I was starving. It seemed as if breakfast had been hours and hours ago.

Kate glanced at her watch. "It *is* almost noon. Okay, let's go. And while we're there, we can pick up something for Stephanie's costume, too."

Stephanie looked at me and rolled her eyes.

"At least you won't look like my great aunt Helene," I whispered to her.

"No. Just like a fool in a green sheet!" she whispered back.

*   *   *

52

The mall was only a few blocks from Clothing Classics, so we were there in no time. "What do you want for lunch?" Kate asked as we walked through the entrance to the mall.

"Everything," I answered truthfully.

"How about pizza?" Patti suggested.

Stephanie licked her lips. "Sounds good to me."

The Pizza Palace is one of our favorite places to eat. You can get any kind of pizza you want — pepperoni, sausage, mushroom, onion, meatball, even anchovy (yuck!) — and they always put on tons of cheese. Plus, it's really cheap, which is important if you want to get ice cream afterward.

Another thing that's great about the Pizza Palace is that a lot of kids from school go there. It's totally casual. You can hang out practically forever and nobody bothers you to order something. We're pretty friendly with John, the guy who manages the place — oops, I mean "palace."

That day, the Pizza Palace was packed. "I don't think we're going to find a place to sit," I said. "Do you want to go somewhere else?"

"I think I see Mark and Henry," Patti said. The fact that she's so tall comes in handy when you're trying to find someone in a crowd. "Maybe we can sit with them."

"And maybe you can sit next to Henry," Stephanie teased her.

Patti has a crush on Henry, which is convenient because they sit next to each other at school. Henry likes her, too — I can tell. They're really cute together.

We stepped up to the counter. "Hi, John," I said.

"Hi. What can I get you girls?" he said. "Wait, don't tell me. The usual, right?" We almost always order a double-cheese pizza with pepperoni, meatballs, and olives.

"Uh-huh," I said. "And four small Dr Peppers, please."

"Here are the drinks," John said, sliding them across the counter. "I'll bring over the pizza when it's ready."

"Hey, a couple of people just got up," Patti said. "Let's grab those seats." We hurried over to claim two stools next to Henry and Mark.

"Hi," we all said, practically in unison.

"Hi," Henry replied.

"What's up?" asked Mark.

"We were just over at Clothing Classics getting the stuff for the float," Patti informed them, sliding onto the seat next to Henry. Stephanie grabbed the other one, which left me and Kate standing. I hoped two more seats would open up before the pizza was done. I knew I couldn't possibly eat a slice standing up, without dropping all the meatballs onto the floor.

Henry made a face. "Tell me — how bad is it?"

"Well, you don't have to wear a tie or anything," Kate said.

Henry let out a huge sigh of relief.

"But you do have to wear a blazer and real shoes," Patti said. I'd never seen Henry in anything but T-shirts, sweatshirts, jeans, and high-top sneakers. This was going to be very interesting! "You, too, Mark," Kate added.

Mark didn't seem too thrilled but he didn't complain, either, which was nice. "Wait — didn't you guys get the float yesterday?" he asked us.

Kate nodded eagerly. "It's really big. It's going to look great when we get all the furniture on it."

"If it all goes according to plan," Stephanie reminded her.

Kate got this really disgusted look on her face. "That's right, I forgot," she muttered.

"Forgot what?" Henry asked.

I took a sip of my Dr Pepper. "Well, there are going to be two more people on the float," I told them.

"Great!" said Mark enthusiastically.

Kate and I shook our heads. "Not great," she said.

"Who are they?" Henry asked.

"Ginger Kinkaid and Christy Soames," Patti said.

Mark and Henry looked at each other, then back at us. "What's so awful about that?" Mark asked. "I mean, they're just going to sit there, right?"

I shook my head. "Wrong again!"

Henry looked puzzled. "What do you mean?"

"Ginger thinks she has a better idea for how to organize the float," Kate said quickly. "But we pretty much talked her out of it this morning, so it's nothing to worry about."

Pretty much talked her out of it? I repeated to myself. Kate was crazy if she thought Ginger was going to give up so easily. She seemed just as determined as Kate about directing the float.

"What's her idea?" asked Mark.

Kate waved her hand in the air. "It's completely ridiculous."

"She wants to do something more modern," Stephanie explained. "Instead of Riverhurst fifty years ago, she wants to do Riverhurst today, or Riverhurst in the future." She sounded almost wistful.

"I get it — kind of like *Back to the Future, Part Six*," Henry said. "Actually, it might be kind of cool to do Riverhurst today. That way I could just wear what I've got on now!"

Kate frowned at him. "I don't think so," she said, pointing at the ripped knee of his jeans.

"Well, at least it would be authentic!" Patti said, laughing.

"Yeah, and if we did the future, I could wear my 3-D glasses!" Mark added.

Kate had that "I'm about to explode" look again. "Come on, guys. You're not seriously considering Ginger's idea, are you?" she demanded.

"No, I guess not." Henry took a sip of his drink. "The idea's not so terrible, but working with Ginger would be. Remember when we had to work on those special studies projects with the other classes? I got stuck in her group." He shook his head. "Talk about a nightmare. She made us do all the work. Then she presented it to the teachers like it was all *her* project."

"I wouldn't want to work with her either," Mark agreed.

"What do you mean, work with her — work *for* her is more like it," Henry said. "She treats everyone like they're her slaves or something. And Christy's almost as bad."

Patti nodded. "Ginger does tend to act like a bulldozer," she said.

But the image of the bulldozer reminded me more of the way *Kate* was acting about the float. She was pushing ahead with her idea, not even listening to a word we said — though of course I didn't add *that* to the conversation.

"Look, don't worry about Ginger," Kate went on. "We're going ahead as planned. If Ginger and

Christy don't like our idea, they don't have to be on the float. It's as simple as that."

Not when Ginger's uncle was sponsoring *our* float, I added to myself. It wasn't simple at all.

When our pizza arrived, Mark and Henry left. After we ate, we decided to head over to Just Juniors, this clothing store that sells all the latest and greatest looks.

As we walked into the store, Kate froze in her tracks. "Do you see what I see?" she said. She pointed to the left side of the store, where the dressing rooms are located.

Ginger was standing in front of the three-way mirror. She had on a lime-green miniskirt and was twirling around, studying her reflection. Ginger isn't pretty, exactly, but she is interesting-looking.

Christy came out of the dressing room wearing the same skirt, in a bright neon pink.

"Don't tell me," Kate whispered.

We moved a little closer, hiding behind a big table piled high with sweaters.

"Those new rubber miniskirts are selling like wild," Lucy, the manager of Just Juniors, told Ginger and Christy.

"A skirt made out of rubber?" I said, confused. "Do you wear them in the rain or what?"

Stephanie and Patti giggled.

"They're the hottest look around," Lucy continued as Christy admired herself in the mirror. Naturally, the skirt looked fantastic on Christy. But then, she would look good in a burlap sack!

"You know what, Christy? These will be just perfect for the float!" Ginger squealed.

Uh-oh, I said to myself. I was right — Ginger hadn't given up any more than Kate had. They were both charging full steam ahead with their ideas.

"A rubber miniskirt on my float!" Kate said in a choked voice. "No way. Ginger Kinkaid is not going to push us around!" She turned and stormed out of the store.

"So much for shopping," Stephanie murmured as we followed Kate out of the mall. "And I know Kate would kill me for saying this, but those skirts looked really good on them."

Patti sighed. "Better than a bubble-gum pink sweater with a jumbo flower on it, that's for sure."

"Yeah, even if they are made out of rubber!" I added.

Chapter 6

I spent the rest of Saturday cleaning my room. Believe me, it took all afternoon. And when I was finished, it still didn't look that good. That night my parents had some friends over for dinner, so I rented a movie and watched it by myself. Not exactly a thrilling Saturday night, but this morning had been exciting enough. Besides, Stephanie was baby-sitting her baby brother and sister, and Patti was working on something for the Quarks — a science club at school she belongs to. Kate was going out to dinner with her family. So it was me and Tom Cruise, all alone for once. Actually, I wasn't *all* alone. Rocky was snuggled up against me. But he isn't a very good conversationalist.

Instead of enjoying the movie, though, I kept thinking about the argument between Ginger and Kate that morning. We had plans to work on the float

Sunday afternoon, and I had a nasty feeling Ginger was going to drop by again and who knew what would happen then? It was strange. Usually I'm one thousand percent behind Kate's ideas. But this time . . . Ginger's idea for making the float more modern was a pretty good one . . . maybe even better than Kate's!

But I could never tell Kate that. Kate was acting like this was war — and if I chose Ginger's side, I'd be the enemy. In fact, Kate probably wouldn't even forgive me, not in a million years.

But I thought she was being kind of unreasonable about the whole thing. Ginger *was* acting obnoxious, but that's just the way she is. Besides, Kate wasn't acting any better. I didn't have to be best friends with Ginger or anything, but I thought her idea would be fun to work on. And I could tell that Stephanie liked it, too. Who wouldn't like to dress up in cool, trendy clothes? At least students from fifty years ago probably got to *choose* what they wore!

But what could we do? Kate wasn't going to give up, and neither was Ginger. Neither one was exactly the compromising type.

The way things were going, I thought glumly, we probably *would* end up cutting the float in half!

"How's your float going?" my father asked cheerfully the next morning at breakfast. "I forgot to ask you last night. Making any progress?"

I wasn't quite sure how to answer that question. "Well, uh, we know, uh, which clothes we're going to get," I stammered. "Or at least I think so. We're going to work on it some more this afternoon, right, Roger?"

My brother nodded, his mouth full of pancake. "Linda's coming over, too." Linda is Roger's girl-friend. She's really pretty, and she's nice, too.

"Is there anything I can do to help?" my mother asked.

"Well, actually, we *do* need someone to pick up the desks at the antique store," I told her.

"No, you don't," Roger corrected me.

I looked at him. "Why not?"

"Because I found some old desks at school for you. They're the same ones that used to be in your school," Roger explained. "I asked one of the custodians if there were any old desks lying around, and he told me there were a whole bunch in the basement."

"You're kidding! You mean, the desks were actually in Riverhurst School fifty years ago?"

"They're the real thing," Roger said.

"Thanks!" I said. "That's excellent. Now our float will be totally authentic." I knew Kate would like that. "What do you think they were saving those old desks for?"

Roger shrugged. "You got me. Firewood, maybe. Anyway, he's going to let me have them tomorrow. I'll bring them home with me after school."

"We still need a blackboard, though," I said.

"We can stop by the antique store later this morning and pick that up, okay?" my mother said.

"I saw Ginger Kinkaid outside with you yesterday," my father said. "How is that going?"

"As well as can be expected," I told him truthfully. "She and Kate don't exactly see eye-to-eye on things."

"Uh-oh," my mother said. "Kate does tend to be a bit stubborn."

A bit? I thought to myself. *Majorly* stubborn is more like it.

"Yeah, kind of . . ." I said out loud.

"I'm sure they'll work out their differences by the time the parade comes around," my father said. "Besides, what's there to fight about?"

"Don't ask," I mumbled.

After breakfast it started pouring and it didn't stop all day. We decided to cancel our plans to work on the float, even though it took me about an hour to convince Kate it was too cold and wet to go outside. The float was in the garage, of course, but it can get pretty cold out there. And Patti and Stephanie sure weren't psyched about making the trip over to my house and getting completely drenched. Kate was disappointed. But then I told her about the desks, and she got all excited again.

"Great! Promise me we'll work on the float tomorrow after school?" she said.

"I promise," I said.

It was funny, but that was the first time I actually felt glad Kate and I didn't live next door anymore. I didn't feel like working on the float — I just wanted to lie on my bed and read. I knew that if we still lived on Pine Street, Kate would be at my house night and day trying to get the float ready before Ginger set eyes on it again!

"No, no, that's all wrong!" Kate exclaimed. "You need to hold your arm up much higher!"

Stephanie grunted as she raised her arm. "It's kind of awkward," she said, "especially since I'm holding a rock instead of a candle!"

We were standing outside after school on Monday afternoon. Kate wanted Stephanie to practice posing as The Spirit of Riverhurst statue. I thought she looked fine. But Kate wanted Stephanie to look exactly like the statue.

"Can't I take a break now?" Stephanie asked as Kate walked slowly around her.

"Concentrate," Kate instructed her. "Try to match the expression on her face."

"I can't even see her expression, that statue's so old and worn out," Stephanie wailed.

"You should look serious, but not too serious," Kate said. "You enjoy school so much that it is a *pleasure* to study."

I started to giggle. "Yeah, right!"

Stephanie bit her lip to keep from smiling. Kate was getting so carried away about a stupid statue.

"No, no! That's not it at all!" Kate said sternly. "She's not smiling."

"I give up!" Stephanie cried.

"I think she's close enough," Patti said. "Don't you want to get to Lauren's?" We'd already spent at least fifteen minutes staring at Stephanie and that statue.

"Just a few more minutes," Kate said. "Don't you want to get it just right?"

I had a feeling that was the last thing Stephanie wanted to do just then. But she hoisted the rock back up in the air, focused on the big apple tree across the street, and tried to look serious, but not *too* serious. I knew she probably wouldn't want to hear it, but she was doing a good impression of the statue.

A group of sixth-grade boys came sauntering out the front door of the school. I spotted Taylor Sprouse right away, since he was wearing all black, as usual. Stephanie couldn't see them coming because her back was to them.

"I think she has it now," I said to Kate urgently. "Let's go." I gestured in the direction of Taylor and his friends.

But Kate didn't notice. "Just a second," she said. "What do you think — should her arm be a little higher?"

"Ka-te. We're not going to remember all this by Saturday! Anyway, no one else is going to notice if she's not a hundred percent correct," I pointed out. "Come on, let's go." I tugged at Kate's sleeve.

She didn't budge.

"My arm is getting tired," Stephanie complained. She looked like she wanted to throw that rock at somebody — somebody named Kate Beekman!

"Wooo! Come on guys, take a look!" a voice called out at that moment. It was Taylor. He came and stood right in front of Stephanie. "What have we here?" he said. "Hey — I know — it's Miss Spirit of Riverhurst!" Then he and his friends started to laugh.

Stephanie's face turned bright red and she immediately dropped the rock. It hit her foot and rolled to a stop in front of him. She winced.

"Is that statue your idol or something?" Phil Smith asked, still laughing.

"No," Stephanie muttered.

"We're rehearsing," Kate informed them.

"For what — the statue look-alike contest?"

Taylor joked. "I didn't know there was one. Maybe I'll try to be Abraham Lincoln."

"It's for our Homecoming float," Kate said coolly.

"Now *that* I have to see!" Richard Barrett said.

"Yeah, we'll be watching for you in the parade," Taylor told Stephanie. He and his friends started to walk away. "Goodbye, Miss Spirit of Riverhurst!" he shouted.

Stephanie closed her eyes. "I don't believe that just happened."

"Bad timing," I agreed sympathetically.

"They were really obnoxious," Patti said. "But you know, it says in *Teen Topics* that boys only tease you when they like you. So maybe Taylor likes you."

"If that's true, then he likes you a lot," I added.

Stephanie picked up the rock and started shifting it from hand to hand. "I doubt it," she said gloomily. She closed her eyes again. "I'd like to just disappear for a while — like *forever!*"

"Well, are you ready to go work on the float?" Kate said cheerfully.

Stephanie glared at her. Then she turned and flounced over to the bike rack without another word. Patti and I looked at each other. Didn't Kate even realize how embarrassing that had been for Stephanie? And from what Taylor and his friends had said, this wasn't going to be the end of it, either. They'd probably be calling her "Miss Spirit of Riverhurst" for the next year. What was Kate's problem?

We were just getting on our bikes when the front door opened and a bunch of kids came out.

"Uh-oh, there's Ginger," Kate said. "We'd better make our getaway fast!"

But it was too late. Ginger had already seen us and was hurrying over. And Christy was right by her side, as usual. "Are we going to work on the float this afternoon?" Ginger asked us.

"Well, *we* are," Kate said.

"Great! I'll be over in a little while," Ginger said. "I just have to do a few things first."

"You mean pick up the stuff?" Christy asked.

Ginger gave her a look as if to say "not now."

Oh, no! I thought. Now, we're definitely in for it.

If Ginger was going to show up with the things *she* wanted to put on the float, there was going to be trouble. Big trouble. Ginger obviously knew that, too. But luckily, Kate hadn't heard Christy's comment because she was already halfway down the block, riding away. Kate was probably still planning to get the float finished before Ginger even got to my house!

"So we'll see you later," Ginger said to the rest of us.

"Okay," I said. But I knew it wasn't going to be okay. Not at all!

Chapter
7

"Is this straight?" Roger asked me. He was holding up the Blaney Realty sign on the side of the float.

"A little higher on the left," I told him. "Perfect!"

"Roger, could you put a couple of the desks on the float?" Kate asked.

"Sure thing," he said. He finished nailing the sign onto the side, then picked up a desk and put it on top of the float.

"I love it!" Kate exclaimed.

"That blackboard looks terrific up there, too," Linda, Roger's girlfriend, said. "Oh — I almost forgot. I brought something for you." She picked up a large plastic bag and pulled out a sweater. "I asked my grandmother if she had anything you could use for the float, and she came up with this!" Linda unfolded the sweater — it was an old varsity letter sweater with a big letter "R" on it.

"Is that a real Riverhurst High letter sweater?" Stephanie asked.

"It was my grandfather's," Linda said. "I thought one of you could wear it."

"This is great," Kate said, running her hands over the letter. "Thanks, Linda. I promise we'll be really careful with it."

"Can I wear it?" Patti asked eagerly.

"No, this is for one of the boys. Besides, you have that other great sweater to wear!" Kate reminded her.

Patti raised an eyebrow. "Right. I forgot."

I got up on the float and stood in front of the blackboard. "What should we write on this?"

"How about 'Kick me'?" Roger suggested as he lifted another desk onto the float. "Or, 'I will not chew gum in class' — one hundred times." He and Linda laughed.

"No. That wouldn't be appropriate," Kate said. Appropriate? She didn't seem to realize that Roger was only kidding.

"What about the date?" Patti said. "You know how some teachers write 'Today's Date' in the corner of the board every day?"

"Good idea!" Kate said. "That'll take care of the calendar we wanted to do, too." She jumped up onto the float beside me. "I'll write it," she said, taking the chalk out of my hand.

"You know, Kate, I can write, too," I told her. I was getting pretty fed up with Kate Beekman, Director of Everything!

"Oh, I know," Kate said. "But I know just how it should look!" She wrote the date in big script on the board. It didn't even look that good — I could have done better, and my handwriting's awful! "There!" she said with satisfaction. She turned to Patti. "Patti, come up here. I want to see how it looks when people are sitting at the desks. Lauren, you sit beside her."

"Aye-aye, sir," I mumbled under my breath.

"Of course on the real float, you and Henry will sit here," Kate informed Patti. "Now, places please."

Patti and I sat down at the desks and tried to look serious. I felt like an idiot. Then I pictured myself wearing that awful yellow blouse and trying to look serious — it was a frightening thought.

"I think it would be funny if Henry was fooling around in class," I suggested.

"You mean acting like himself?" Patti said, grinning. Henry is famous for getting into trouble for not paying attention and not doing his homework. And he comes up with the craziest excuses in the world.

"No, kids didn't fool around in class back then," Kate replied.

"I don't know about that," Roger said. "I think

there's always at least one class clown, no matter where you are."

"Maybe, but it's not right for this float," Kate said positively. "Now, Stephanie, you'll be up front, of course. That reminds me — we forgot to pick up a sheet for you at the mall."

"That's okay," Stephanie said glumly. She climbed up onto the float.

Kate stopped walking around and looked at Stephanie. "Are you feeling all right?"

"Sure," Stephanie answered.

"You sound kind of tired," Kate said. "Are you sure you're not coming down with the chicken pox? Fatigue is one of the first symptoms, you know."

Personally, I thought Stephanie was just tired of hearing about how she was going to have to wear a sheet — a *green* sheet, no less — in front of the whole town. Besides, she had just experienced one of the most embarrassing moments of her life. That can take a lot out of a person. Plus, she'd dropped a big rock on her foot!

"I feel fine," Stephanie told Kate. "Really." Then she started scratching her arm.

Kate's jaw dropped. "Stephanie!" she cried. "You do have it!"

Stephanie grinned. "No. I was just teasing you." She pulled up the sleeve of her sweatshirt. "See — no red bumps." Then she did a comical pose on the front of the float — she looked like she was about to leap off of it.

Patti and I laughed, but Kate glared at us. "It's not funny. Stephanie can't come down with the chicken pox. We need her for this float to be absolutely perfect."

"Are they giving out awards?" Linda asked.

"Not that I know of," Kate said.

"That's too bad. You'd probably have a good shot at winning."

I sighed. That was all Kate needed to hear. If she got any more determined to make the float the best ever, she'd probably drive us all completely out of our minds!

"Lauren, would you come here for a minute?" my mother called out the front door.

"Coming!" I hopped off the float and ran to the house.

"Follow me," my mother said, leading me into the kitchen just as the oven timer went off. She took a sheet of oatmeal-butterscotch chip cookies out of the oven and slipped them onto a large plate. "I thought you all could use some refreshment seeing as you're working so hard," she said, handing me a stack of napkins. "Be careful — they're hot!"

I blew on one to cool it off as I walked outside. When I stepped out the front door, Ginger was walking up the driveway. She was carrying a big bag.

"Uh, hi, Ginger," I said as cheerfully as I could. "Would you like a cookie? They just came out of the oven."

"What kind are they?" Ginger asked.

"They're Scotchies," I told her, taking a bite. "Mmm . . . delish."

"No thank you," Ginger said, peering into the garage. "I'm not wild about butterscotch."

"So, where's Christy?" I asked, hoping to stall her.

"She had to go to the dentist," Ginger said.

"Uh, what's in the bag? Did you go shopping?" I went on. "Buy a new sweater or something?"

Ginger didn't answer. She just kept walking toward the garage. I heaved a loud sigh, then took another bite of my cookie. I had a feeling it was going to be a long afternoon.

"Hey! What's going on?" Ginger demanded, setting her bag down on the edge of the float.

"We're getting the float ready," Kate said.

"What's that blackboard doing up there?" Ginger asked.

"It kind of goes with the desks," Roger said, giving her a strange look.

Ginger tapped her foot against the concrete floor. "Well, we're not using those desks anymore, are we?"

"Why wouldn't we be?" Kate asked. She crossed

her arms over her chest. "We *told* you, this float is going to be Riverhurst School fifty years ago."

"And *I* told *you* I thought that was a bad idea," Ginger shot back. "We decided to go with a more updated look."

"No, *we* didn't. *You* did," said Kate.

"Do something," Patti mouthed to me. I don't know why she expected *me* to know what to do. She's usually the peacemaker in our group.

"Um, guys, look. Let's not fight about it," I cut in. "Umm, does anyone want a cookie? They're yummy." No one answered. I put the plate down on top of the float. So much for the eat-a-cookie-and-forget-about-it tactic!

"You're right, Lauren. We shouldn't fight about it — because it's *my* decision what goes on this float," Ginger said firmly.

"What?" Kate cried, hopping down off the float. "It's not your decision! We're the ones who planned the whole thing. You just jumped in at the last minute," she said angrily.

"Well, I think you should at least listen to my idea. After all, it's *my uncle's* float," Ginger retorted. "If I ask him, he'll do whatever I want."

"Oh, yeah? Well, your uncle already approved *our* idea, not yours," Kate shot back. "Anyway, your idea's stupid!"

"Not as stupid as dressing like a bunch of old

ladies!" Ginger yelled. "The whole town is going to be laughing at you!"

Kate gritted her teeth. "Oh, yeah? Don't you think they'd laugh at you in your dumb rubber mini-skirt?" she said.

"How do you know about that?" Ginger asked.

"We saw you at the mall, so don't think we don't know what you've been up to," Kate said. "You can just forget it. The day we let you ruin our float is the day I die!"

I didn't like the way Kate kept saying "we" and "our float." She'd been acting all along like it was *her* float — especially today. She hadn't listened to any of our objections, and she wasn't even trying to compromise with Ginger. Being stubborn is one thing — pigheaded is another!

"Oh, yeah?" Ginger was saying. "Well, the day I dress up in ugly fifty-year-old clothes is the day *I* die!"

"It's been nice knowing you," Kate said.

Ginger grabbed her bag. "I'm going to talk to my uncle about this!" she declared. She turned and stalked angrily down the driveway.

"Now I know what you meant when you said they didn't see eye-to-eye," Roger whispered in my ear.

I nodded slowly. I was getting pretty angry myself, and not at Ginger, either. "Kate," I said, "you shouldn't have done that."

"Why not?" she replied, frowning at me.

"Because!" I threw up my hands. "Mr. Blaney's the one who's sponsoring our float. If Ginger tells him we won't even consider her idea, he might cancel the whole thing!"

"So what did you want me to do?" Kate said crossly. "Just go along with her dumb idea?"

"I don't see what's so dumb about it," Stephanie commented.

Kate whirled around and stared at her. "What do you mean?"

"I just think maybe you should have listened to her idea," Stephanie said.

"You didn't even give her a chance," I added.

"Why should I?" Kate demanded.

I took a deep breath and braced myself. I didn't usually disagree with Kate, and I knew she wasn't going to like it. "Because you're not the only one in the world with good ideas!" I said. "And you keep ordering us around like we don't know how to do anything. You act like we can't even lift a finger to help with the float because we might mess it up! I thought this was supposed to be *our* project, not *yours*!"

There was a tense silence in the garage. I felt

sorry for Linda and Roger, who were sort of trapped there.

"Are you saying you think her idea is *better* than mine?!" Kate asked, looking at me as if I had lost my mind.

"Some of it was," I replied.

"It would be sort of nice to dress like students of the future instead of the ancient past," Stephanie said wistfully.

"The computers might look really cool," Patti put in.

"So what you're all really saying is you think her idea *is* better than mine!" Kate said accusingly.

Stephanie shrugged. "Well, maybe a float all about what school was like fifty years ago *is* a little dull. Maybe we should think about changing it."

"I wouldn't mind changing it a *little*," Kate said. "But Ginger doesn't want to compromise. She wants it to be totally her float. She's impossible to work with!"

"Talk about not compromising!" I burst out. "Kate, you've been doing everything *your* way! It's like we're not even here! You're making Stephanie dress up like a statue — even though she hates it — and you wouldn't even let Patti and I decide what we were going to wear! You're the one who's impossible to work with!"

That was probably the longest speech I had ever

made in my whole life! I didn't know I was so angry with her until I started talking — and then everything just came pouring out.

Kate was staring at me, a shocked expression on her face. She wasn't used to me standing up to her. In fact, it had never really happened before. I don't usually mind Kate being a little bossy, but this was different. She was overdoing it.

Kate shrugged angrily and her lower lip trembled. "Well, Lauren, if you don't like the way I'm doing it, why don't you just do the float yourself!" She was acting tough, but I could tell she was trying hard not to cry. "I hereby *resign* as float director," she said in a wobbly voice. "Go ahead, do whatever you want. I don't even want to be on the stupid old thing! I'm sure *I'd* just ruin it!"

She ran out of the garage and got on her bike. Then she turned back to me and yelled, "I'll never forget what you said to me, Lauren Hunter, and I'll never forgive you, either!"

Then she was gone.

Chapter
8

I couldn't believe it. Kate and I had had our first major fight. Oh, sure, we'd had little arguments before. We'd even gone without speaking for an hour or two. But we'd never blown up at each other like this. I felt horrible.

Stephanie and Patti assured me she'd get over it, but somehow I wasn't so sure. Maybe, just maybe, our friendship was really over. . . . And if it was, what about the Sleepover Friends?

That night I couldn't do anything except think about Kate. I was supposed to be working on a big science report, but I didn't have the energy. I couldn't figure out what was supposed to go in Column A and what was supposed to go in Column B. "If Kate were here I'd know where to start," I said out loud. That made me even sadder.

I tossed my notebook on the floor and lay down on my bed.

"M-reow!" Rocky jumped off the bed.

"I'm sorry, Rocky — I didn't know you were there," I said. I picked him up and started stroking his fur.

"Remember that girl who was always over here?" I asked him gloomily. "The short blonde one? Well, you probably won't ever see her again."

Rocky meowed.

"I know — I don't like it, either," I said. But what could I do? I had to tell Kate that the way she was acting was driving us crazy. Weren't friends supposed to be able to criticize each other? Maybe I'd just read that in some dumb magazine.

What was I going to do without Kate? I wondered. Who would tell me how to organize my homework? Who would tell me to stop dreaming and get my head out of the clouds? Who would call me The Bottomless Pit? Okay, so it wasn't the nicest nickname in the world — but it was Kate's.

We'd been friends since kindergarten. We'd played about a hundred million games of Truth or Dare and we knew all each other's secrets. We'd slept over at each other's house every Friday night for years . . . we'd even had the chicken pox, the measles, and the mumps together. I was never going to find another friend like Kate. Ever.

"Well, Rocky," I said, scratching him beneath the chin. "It's just you and me, kid."

My mother practically had to shake me out of bed the next morning. I definitely didn't feel like going to school. In fact, I wasn't sure I wanted to go to school ever again. Kate was going to ignore me, and I wasn't going to talk to her, either. It was going to be miserable.

I stumbled out the front door about ten minutes later than usual. Then I took a second look. Someone was waiting at the end of the driveway.

"Kate?" I called softly.

She rode up on her bike. "Hi," she said shyly.

"How did you get here?" I asked.

"My mom drove me over," she explained. "Lauren, I'm sorry about what happened yesterday."

"So am I," I said, climbing onto my bike. But I wasn't going to take back what I said — I knew that I meant every word of it.

"I was up almost all night, thinking. I thought about what I said to Ginger. . . . You were right — I was being unreasonable," Kate said. "To all of you, not just Ginger."

I practically fell over on my bike. Kate — apologizing for being stubborn? This was definitely a first.

"I know I get too bossy sometimes," she went

on. "I don't mean to be — I just get wrapped up in what I'm doing. Then I start telling people what to do. I guess I get so excited about things and I forget to be nice."

I nodded. "That's okay."

"Is it?" she said, looking at me hopefully.

I shrugged my shoulders. "I know you don't mean to do it," I said. "You just get carried away with your ideas — kind of like me."

"Yeah," Kate said seriously. "I guess we're more alike than I thought. Anyway, I came up with an idea for a compromise. I think you'll like it."

"Go ahead," I said, smiling.

"The more I thought about Ginger's idea, the more I realized she had one good point about the past being sort of boring," Kate explained. "Actually, I guess I thought her idea wasn't *too* bad right from the start. I just didn't want to admit it."

"It was kind of hard to believe that she came up with something good," I agreed. "Who wants to take advice from Ginger Kinkaid? So, what's your idea?"

"Well . . ." Kate said eagerly, "we could show what students have looked like *over* the past fifty years. Instead of just showing the nineteen forties, we can show each decade — the fifties, the sixties, right up to the present! And each of us can dress for a different decade."

"That sounds excellent!" I said, and I meant it. "What about Ginger and Christy?"

"Ginger can be whatever decade she wants. Who cares! I think Christy would make a great student of today, though," Kate said. "That is, if anyone's *really* wearing rubber minis these days. If not, she can represent the future." She giggled.

"What should we call it?" I asked.

"I was thinking 'Riverhurst School Through the Years,' " Kate announced with a flourish.

"Definitely Oscar-winning material," I said, grinning at her.

Kate glanced at her watch. "We're not going to win anything if we don't get to school right now!" she cried. "We have five minutes!"

We rode like crazy straight to school and dashed into class a couple of minutes after the final bell rang.

"Would you two mind telling me why you're late this morning?" Mrs. Mead asked us as we scurried to our seats.

"Um, we were working on the float," I said, panting from our mad dash down the hallway.

"Oh, really? This early? Well, how is it going?" Mrs. Mead inquired.

"Fine!" Kate told her with a polite smile.

I glanced at Stephanie and Patti — they were staring at us as if they couldn't believe their eyes.

The last thing they knew, Kate had resigned as float director and sworn she would never forgive me as long as she lived!

"It's going to be a great float," I said to Mrs. Mead.

"I'm glad. Now, do you think you could forget the float and concentrate on some arithmetic?" Mrs. Mead turned around and started writing long-division problems on the blackboard.

I grinned at Kate. We were a team again!

At noon, after we got our lunches, Kate apologized to Patti and Stephanie and asked them what they thought about the new plan.

Stephanie's eyes grew wide with excitement as Kate described it. "You mean we all get to wear normal clothes?" she asked.

Kate nodded. "No more Miss Spirit of Riverhurst."

"Hooray!" Stephanie threw her fist in the air and practically knocked over her carton of chocolate milk.

"I guess we still have to run it by Ginger," Kate said. "But I think she'll like it." She glanced around the cafeteria. "The only problem is, I don't see her anywhere."

"I don't either," Patti said.

"Look, there's Christy," I said, pointing to the end of the lunch line.

Kate jumped up from her chair. "She'll know where Ginger is."

A few minutes later, Kate came running back toward our table. "You guys aren't going to believe this!" she cried. "Ginger isn't here because . . . she has the chicken pox!"

"Seriously?" Patti asked.

"You're kidding, right?" I said. "I mean, she looked fine yesterday."

Kate waved her hand in the air. "You can come down with it overnight," she said. "Trust me! Anyway, I told Christy to come over here so we could tell her what we'd like to do now."

I stared at Kate, surprised at how well she was handling this.

"Don't look at me like that!" Kate said. "I mean, Mr. Blaney *is* Ginger's uncle. And Christy is Ginger's best friend." She smiled. "A successful director has to know when to humor a temperamental star."

I couldn't help smiling, too. Trust Kate to put it in filmmaking terms!

"Shh! Here she comes," Stephanie warned.

"Did Kate tell you about Ginger?" Christy set her tray down on our table and slid into a chair. "It's just awful, isn't it?"

"Yes, it is too bad," Patti said.

"I hope she doesn't get any scars," Christy continued. "That would be *so* terrible." She sipped her milk. "She's going to be really upset about missing the parade."

"Maybe she'll be better by then," Patti said.

"Anyway, I wanted to tell you about my new plan for the float," Kate said. "I've — I mean, we've — decided we should go for a more modern look."

"We could call it 'Riverhurst School Through the Years,' " I said. "And each of us could dress up like a student from a different decade."

"Hmm. Not bad. Not bad at all," Christy said. "I hope you have fun."

Kate looked at me, and I looked at Stephanie, and then Patti.

"What do you mean, Christy?" Patti asked. "Aren't you going to be on it, too?"

"Well," Christy said thoughtfully, "I doubt it."

"But, Christy," Kate said, "we want you to wear one of those rubber minis. You'd be perfect as the student of today — you know, wearing all the latest clothes and everything."

Christy smiled. "I have earrings and a big bracelet to match that skirt," she said. "Maybe one of you could borrow them."

"I don't get it," I said. "Why aren't you going to wear them?"

Christy shook her head. "I can't be on the float if Ginger's not going to be."

"Why not?" Stephanie asked.

Christy didn't answer right away. "It wouldn't be right. She's my best friend," she finally said. "Since she can't do it, I shouldn't either. Also, well, although your new plan is pretty good, I don't want Ginger to think I'm, you know, on your side or something."

"But that's not fair," Patti said. "It's not a question of sides. We should all be in this together."

"Yeah, *you* don't have the chicken pox," Stephanie pointed out. "And Kate has already compromised. Ginger should, too."

"I know," Christy said. "But she's my best friend. I have to stick by her."

"Not when she's being unfair!" Stephanie argued. "Look, if she was really your friend, she'd *want* you to be on the float and have fun even if she is home sick."

"Stephanie's right," Patti said. "We changed our plan so you guys would ride, too. You can't just back out now."

I glanced nervously over at Kate, but she was smiling.

"Maybe you're right," Christy said.

"We know we're right," I said confidently. "We

need you, Christy. I mean, this is going to be like a fashion show."

Christy giggled. "I guess it wouldn't hurt for me to ride on the float," she said. "Since it's still partly Ginger's idea and all."

"All right!" Stephanie said. "One chic float, coming up!"

Chapter
9

"Even the woman at Clothing Classics thought it was a good idea!" Kate said triumphantly. She sat down at the lunch table with the rest of us. "She wants us to make a list of the *new* things we need, with sizes. I told her I'd go over there after school."

"I can come, too," I volunteered.

"Thanks," Kate said. "I might need some help carrying the stuff to my house."

Mark and Henry stopped by our table. "What's going on with the float?" Mark asked. "What did you mean when you told Mrs. Mead it was much better?"

"We've decided to change it around," Kate told them.

"Ginger isn't in charge, now, is she?" Henry whispered to me.

I shook my head. "No. She has the chicken pox."

"So what's the story?" Henry asked.

"Instead of showing what the school was like fifty years ago, we're going to show what it was like twenty years ago, and ten years ago, and forty years ago, too." Kate explained in a rush. Then she turned to Christy. "We're also going to show what students look like today. And now we have to decide what we're all going to wear!" She picked up a clean napkin from her tray and unfolded it. "Does anyone have a pen?" Typical Kate — making another list.

"I do," Henry said.

Kate made three columns: Year, Person, Clothes. "Okay, who wants to dress in something from the forties?"

Stephanie suddenly became very interested in her lunch. I took a long sip of my orange juice, and Patti stared at her sneakers.

Kate grinned. "Okay, okay. I'll do it." She wrote down: "letter sweater, and skirt, saddle shoes." I noticed that she'd even given up on the rose sweater and the ugly yellow blouse!

Henry and Patti volunteered for the fifties. Henry was going to wear a leather jacket and jeans, and slick his hair back. "Just like Elvis," he said happily. Patti was going to wear a poodle skirt — whatever that was — and saddle shoes and a cardigan sweater.

I ended up being chosen for the sixties because everyone said I had the right haircut. I would be parading through town in a black blouse, a miniskirt, and white go-go boots. I was kind of afraid I'd end up looking like my mom's old Barbie doll, but Christy told me the look was "totally now!" Mark was also going to be a sixties student. He'd be wearing bell-bottoms and something called a Nehru jacket. Kate said everyone wore them in the sixties movies and we'd just have to trust her.

"And that leaves the seventies for you," Kate told Stephanie. "Which is perfect, because you have long hair."

"I'm not going to have to wear one of those disco outfits, am I?" Stephanie asked suspiciously. "You know, those icky polyester shirts with the big lapels and white pants?"

We all started laughing. "From Miss Spirit of Riverhurst to Miss Lounge Lizard!" I cried.

"Stephanie, did you ever see *Saturday Night Fever*?" Kate asked solemnly. "I want you to look exactly like that!"

"Come on, this isn't funny." Stephanie pouted as Kate started to giggle. "Why do I always get stuck with the worst part?"

"Hey — I have to wear bell-bottoms," Mark reminded her.

"I have an idea. Let Stephanie wear clothes from the *early* seventies," Christy suggested. "All that stuff is kind of in right now, anyway."

"Like what?" Kate asked.

"Tie-dyed shirts, old jeans with patches all over them, big silver hoop earrings — you know," Christy said.

"Oh, please, please, please, let me wear that instead," Stephanie begged Kate. "I'll be the best representative of the early seventies you've ever seen. I'll even wear one of those bandanna headbands. Just don't make me go disco with gold chains and tacky platform shoes!"

"Okay," Kate agreed with a smile. She wrote down the list of clothes she needed to get for Stephanie's outfit.

"Then we're all set!" Stephanie whooped, thrilled with her new part — and her new costume.

"Not quite," said Kate. "We'll have to make some adjustments with the props."

"I think the computer is a good idea," I said hesitantly, hoping Kate wouldn't get mad at me for bringing up one of Ginger's suggestions. "We could put it next to Christy, to symbolize today's student."

"As long as I don't have to work on it!" Christy joked.

"We can borrow my brother's," I said. I hoped he wouldn't mind.

"Okay," Kate agreed. "I'll still carry old books, though."

"The sixties people should carry protest signs," Patti said.

"How about 'Down with School'?" Henry recommended. "Or, even better, 'Down with Homework'?" It figured that was the thing Henry would want to protest!

"We'll have to think about that one," Kate said seriously as the bell rang. "But I like the basic concept."

There she was, sounding just like a movie director. But it didn't bother me anymore. I was glad she was directing the float again. We could never have gotten everything organized like she had. What's more, now she was actually letting everyone participate.

For a second I thought about Ginger, who was lying in bed at home, probably feeling miserable.

It was funny, but I knew that if she were around, things wouldn't be working out as well as they were — one director was enough! But I couldn't help feeling a *little* sorry for her.

Maybe she'd be better by the time of the parade so she could at least see the float. Then again, maybe it would be better if she *wasn't,* I thought.

In any case, I was positive that ours was going to be the absolute best float in the Homecoming parade!

* * *

Now that we'd finally figured out what we were going to do, we got the float ready in no time! Mr. Blaney loved our new idea and he approved it one hundred percent. We were lucky to have such an easygoing person sponsoring us.

It took me about half an hour to get ready for school on Friday morning. It was tour day and Mrs. Mead had told us to look our best. She also said we had to be on our best behavior. The way she was acting, you'd have thought the President of the United States was visiting our school!

I put on my good blue wool pants and a white mock turtleneck sweater. It was kind of cold outside. I hoped it would warm up by tomorrow, since I'd be standing around in a mini all day! I also hoped it wouldn't rain. After all our work, it just couldn't! Could it?

Since we were more dressed up than usual, Mrs. Jenkins gave the four of us a ride to school. When we pulled up in front, there was a big banner on the front door that read "Welcome Back!"

"It doesn't feel like we've been gone very long," I joked.

"Can you imagine us, coming back for our fifty-year reunion?" Kate asked. She opened the door and we climbed out of the backseat. "At least we'll definitely be able to spot Stephanie right away," she said, pointing at Stephanie's outfit. She was wearing a black skirt and a red-and-black vest over a white blouse.

"And you'll probably be *running* the reunion," Stephanie shot back as she got out of the car.

"If she can find time between making big Hollywood movies," I added, grinning at Kate.

"And if Ginger doesn't decide she wants to run it instead," Patti put in. "Thanks for the ride, Mom!"

"Thanks, Mrs. Jenkins!" we all said.

"Have fun today, and I'll see you tonight!" Mrs. Jenkins waved at us as she drove off.

Our sleepover that night was going to be at Patti's house. Kate was going to bring all the clothes for the parade, so we could have a dress rehearsal, and also because we'd be leaving from Patti's house the next morning. The parade didn't start until eleven o'clock, but we had to be there an hour earlier to get in line with the rest of the floats. Roger was going to pull our float behind his car.

When we walked into the school, I couldn't believe my eyes. It was jammed with people!

"Wow! I didn't expect people to get here so early," Patti exclaimed.

"Neither did I," said Kate. "Look — isn't that Mrs. Dexter?" Mrs. Dexter lives on Pine Street, near Kate's house. She's retired and lives alone. She used to baby-sit for us when we were little and she makes the most unbelievable butterscotch brownies I've ever tasted.

"Let's go say hello," I said to Kate. "I haven't seen her since I moved." We headed over to Mrs. Dexter, who was chatting with a group of other people her age who I didn't know.

"Hi, Mrs. Dexter," I said.

"Lauren! Kate! Stephanie! Patti! It's so nice to see you all." Mrs. Dexter reached over and gave us each a hug.

"I forgot that you'd be here today," Kate admitted.

"It's not like you to forget anything, Kate," Mrs. Dexter winked at me. "I wouldn't miss this for the world. You know, I was in the first class to graduate from Riverhurst High School."

"Really?" I said. "That's neat. Are you going to visit our class?"

"Certainly," Mrs. Dexter answered. "I have to make sure you girls are staying on your toes, don't I?"

"We have a float in the parade tomorrow," Kate told her.

"So your mother told me." Mrs. Dexter put her hand on Kate's shoulder. "Is it going to be the best one?" She's always encouraging us to do our best.

Kate nodded. "Definitely."

"I'll be there," Mrs. Dexter assured us. "I think I'll catch up with some of my old classmates now. Some of them came from as far away as Hawaii!"

"Okay, see you later!" I said. I looked around the crowded hallway to see if there was anyone else I knew.

Just then the bell rang. Kate, Stephanie, Patti, and I turned and tried to hurry down the hallway. "At least we have a good excuse for being late," I said, gently squeezing my way past a large group of people wearing nametags.

"Yeah," Kate agreed. "A traffic jam!"

Chapter
10

That evening after dinner, I went straight over to Patti's house with all my stuff. We had agreed to meet there before the Riverhurst High basketball game, so afterward we could just go back to Patti's and crash.

Patti's little brother Horace answered the door. Horace is only six, but he's incredibly smart — in fact, sometimes I think his brain's already been to college.

"Hi, Horace," I said cheerfully. "What's up?"

"Why can't I be on the float?" he whined.

"There's not enough room," I told him truthfully. "Don't worry, you'll be on lots of floats when you get older."

"Really?" he said doubtfully.

I ruffled his hair. "Really. You'll come to the parade, won't you?"

"Sure," Horace answered. "Patti's upstairs with another girl."

"Stephanie or Kate?" I asked him.

"Neither," he replied. "Someone else."

Confused, I picked up my stuff and climbed the stairs to Patti's bedroom. I opened the door cautiously. "Patti?"

"Hi!" she said. "Come on in! Put down your stuff."

"Hi, Lauren," Christy said.

"Yeah, uh, hi," I said. Even though we'd been spending a lot of time with Christy lately, rehearsing the float, I was still amazed to see her at one of our sleepovers! We almost never invite anyone else, except Bitsy Barton once or twice.

"I brought some makeup for us to wear, since we're supposed to be high school students. I borrowed some lipstick from my mom, and some eyeshadow, and — " Christy looked around the room — "Oops, I think I left my pocketbook downstairs."

"You'd better find it before my brother does," Patti warned. "He'll turn it inside out!"

Christy left the room and I heard her dash down the stairs.

"I had to invite her," Patti explained once Christy was gone. "It just didn't seem right not to, since we've done everything for the float together and we're all going to get ready here tomorrow morning."

"That's okay," I said. "I was just a little surprised."

"Shocked, you mean," Patti said, smiling.

I put down my small suitcase and sleeping bag. "Actually, I can take Christy okay by herself. It's when she and Ginger get together that I can't stand."

I was thinking about the time I had invited Ginger to one of our sleepovers, when she first moved to town. Ginger and Kate had disagreed on everything and we'd ended up splitting into two groups and sleeping in separate rooms. I hoped this time wouldn't be such a disaster. But what was Kate going to say? Well, there wasn't anything I could do about it now. At least this way, I knew we'd *look* our best the next morning!

The doorbell rang downstairs, and we heard Christy say hi to Kate and Stephanie. Mrs. Beekman had given them both a ride over.

Patti crossed her fingers as we listened to them come upstairs. Kate, Stephanie, and Christy spilled into the room. "Found it!" Christy announced, holding up her pocketbook.

"Hi, guys," I said.

"Sorry we're late," Kate said. "Melissa the Monster struck again."

"What did she do this time?" Patti asked.

"You know the skirt I'm wearing tomorrow?" Kate said, frowning. "She borrowed it to play dress up, and she got lipstick all over it. I could have killed her! Mom and I spent half an hour trying to get it out."

"Did you?" I asked. Our clothes were only on loan from Clothing Classics, and we'd have to pay for any that we damaged.

"Pretty much," Kate said. "No one will notice tomorrow in the parade, anyway. But I might have to buy it from the store."

"That's too bad," Christy said. "Maybe your parents will pitch in, since it wasn't your fault."

"Good idea," Kate said. "I think I'll ask them."

"I know how you feel," Christy went on. "My little brother Jeffrey can be such a pain!"

Kate rolled her eyes. "Tell me about it!"

I smiled with relief. Kate and Christy could trade little sister and brother horror stories all night.

"We'd better get going," Stephanie said. "We don't want to miss the start of the game. I love it when they introduce the players."

"Oh, I know! Aren't basketball players always the cutest?" Christy added.

"Especially Roger Hunter," Kate said, nudging me with her elbow.

"Who's he?" Christy asked.

"Lauren's brother," Patti said. "And he's the best player on the team, too."

"Come on, girls — time to go!" Mr. Jenkins shouted up the stairs.

"I still can't believe Roger's your brother," Christy said after the game. "He's, like, a real superstar!"

Roger *had* done pretty well in the game. He scored twenty-one points, and led Riverhurst to a 66–54 win. But I wasn't surprised. He practices every chance he gets.

We walked out of the gym and down the hall toward the main entrance, where we were meeting Mr. Jenkins. "Can you believe we'll actually be going here some day?" Patti said.

The high school was so big, it made *me* feel very small.

"I can't wait!" Stephanie said.

"Me neither!" added Christy. "I'll be able to wear makeup then."

We all laughed. "At least that's something to look forward to," Patti said.

When we got back to Patti's house, we grabbed some munchies and headed upstairs. "It might be kind of crowded in here," Stephanie said, looking around Patti's room. It's kind of small and Patti has a double bed, which takes up a lot of room.

"Don't worry — everything's all set up in the attic," Patti said. "We already moved some mattresses up there. We just have to bring up your stuff."

Everyone grabbed the bags and we clambered up the attic stairs. Patti carried a plate of chocolate-chip cookies, a six-pack of Dr Pepper, and a bag of tortilla chips.

"This is cool!" Christy said. "But isn't it dusty?" The Jenkins' attic is very country-looking — it has a pointed ceiling and big oak rafters, and four small round windows. There's just one light bulb that dangles from the ceiling, which makes it kind of dark and creepy. It's the perfect place for telling ghost stories.

"I think it'll be okay," I said.

"If we're going to do a dress rehearsal, we'll need more light," Stephanie said, unpacking her bag. "Want me to get the lamp in your room, Patti?"

"Sure, and bring the full-length mirror, too," Patti suggested. She set the food down in the middle of the floor. "Anyone want a Dr Pepper?"

"Me," I said. She handed me a can.

"I think we should start with the forties and work our way forward," Kate said. "So I'll go downstairs and get ready. Then I'll model for you." She took her clothes out of her suitcase and shook the wrinkles out. "At least Melissa didn't do anything to Linda's grandmother's letter sweater. Be right back!"

Kate went downstairs and Stephanie came back up with the lamp and mirror. We set them up in the corner. A few minutes later Kate made her entrance.

"Ta da!" she said, twirling around in front of us. "So, do I look like I'm from the forties?"

"Actually, you kind of look like you *are* forty," Stephanie giggled.

"I can't help it if they dressed this way!" Kate said.

"I was only kidding," Stephanie said.

"Yeah, don't worry, Kate. The float will be great," Patti reassured her.

"But look at my hair," Kate complained. "I tried to comb it into that wavy style we saw in the old magazines at Clothing Classics, but nothing happened. Instead, I look like I haven't washed it for a week."

I giggled. Kate's hair did look pretty funny. It was sort of sticking out from her head, like it had too much electricity.

"Do you want me to fix it?" Christy asked.

"Can you?" Kate asked.

"I'm pretty good with hairstyles." Christy took a brush and a can of sculpting spray out of her duffel bag. "We can practice tonight, and then you'll know how to fix it tomorrow."

"Can you do mine, too?" I asked. Christy's hair always looks great so I trusted her.

"No problem," she said.

"Christy, can I ask you something? Have you talked to Ginger recently?" Stephanie said.

Christy nodded. "I called her last night."

"How is she?" I asked.

Christy shrugged. "I guess she's feeling better. But she hasn't recovered yet or anything."

"Did you tell her you were going to be on the float?" Kate asked.

"No," Christy said. "I wanted to, but I didn't want her to have a cow. I mean, she *is* sick in bed," she added.

"I guess what she doesn't know won't hurt her. Anyway, it's too late to tell her now, and the parade's tomorrow. . . ." I said.

"I know," Christy nodded. "I'll tell her later, you know, when it's all over. I just hope she doesn't find out by accident, before I can explain."

"Yeah," Kate murmured. "Anyway, if she's not at the parade, I guess she won't find out."

I breathed a sigh of relief. It looked like the parade was going to go off without a hitch. But I crossed my fingers anyway — a little extra luck couldn't hurt.

Chapter
11

The next day was a beautiful day — sunny and warm, without a cloud in the sky.

"Roger's here!" Mr. Jenkins called up the stairway.

The five of us were crowded in front of Patti's mirror, giving our outfits a final once-over. "Are we ready?" Kate asked.

"Ready as we'll ever be," I said, picking a speck of lint off my blouse.

"And I've got the sculpting spray," Christy announced, tucking it into the box-shaped handbag she was carrying as part of her outfit. "In case there are any emergencies."

We raced down the stairs — except for Kate, who had to walk slowly because the saddle shoes she was wearing were a little too big. I heard her mutter something about "these stupid things."

"Whoa," Roger said when we walked outside. "Talk about time travel. Nice threads, guys. What happened to your hair, Lauren? It actually looks good."

"Gee, thanks," I said dryly. He knows how much I hate my stick-straight hair. But Christy had managed to make it look cool and interesting somehow!

"Hop in!" Roger instructed us, opening the back door to his car.

"Can't we ride over on the float?" Kate pleaded.

"No, we'll be going too fast," Roger said.

"Besides, we don't want our hair to get all messed up before the parade even starts," I told Kate.

"Yeah, even *I* don't have that much hair spray," Christy joked.

"Everything looks great up there," Patti said, admiring the float as she climbed into the car. I loved her outfit — the saddle shoes were really cute.

Kate checked her watch. "Only an hour until the parade starts. I think I have a case of terminal butterflies." She glanced up at the float. "Do you think everything will stay in place up there? What if the computer tips over? Or what if Mr. Blaney's sign falls off? He'll never forgive us!"

"Kate?" Roger asked. She didn't answer him at first — she was too wrapped up in worrying about the float. "Kate Beekman!" he said, a little louder. "Come in, please!"

"What?" Kate said.

Roger smiled at her. "Shut up and get in the car, will you?"

"Here we go!" Kate said as the float started moving slowly down the street. "Places, everybody!"

"Hair alert!" I yelled, signaling to Christy.

She ran over and sprayed my bangs a few times. "Okay?"

"I guess so," I said. She ran back to her spot at the rear of the float.

I was so nervous I could feel my knees knocking together. When we turned the corner onto Main Street, all I could see were people — tons of them — standing on the side of the street, waiting for us to pass.

"Why did we ever say we'd do this?" I moaned to Mark over the noise of the marching band in front of us.

Mark just shrugged. He's pretty laid back. He looked pretty funky in his Nehru jacket, but I decided I preferred him in his regular old baseball jacket. He was carrying a protest sign that said "No More Mystery Meat — Improve School Lunches!" That was one cause I definitely supported!

From behind me, Stephanie pulled on my sleeve. "This is great!" she yelled as the band started its next number.

"I don't know . . ." I said. I couldn't get used to the idea of so many people watching *me* and my friends. "I think I've got stage fright!"

"Calm down," Stephanie said. She waved to some people. "This'll be fun!"

After a few more minutes, I got used to the idea of being on stage. Mark and I even started hamming it up a little. When the band broke into an old Beatles song, he and I danced around the edge of the float. I wasn't exactly sure how people danced in the sixties. Mostly, I think they just waved their arms a lot. I had on a necklace with a big silver peace sign on it. It was so big, it was more like a Christmas ornament, and it kept flying around and getting caught in my hair. I didn't care, though. I figured it was all part of the sixties look.

"All *right*, Lauren!" Patti yelled. She and Henry started dancing, too.

Kate looked back at us and crossed her arms over her chest. I thought she was acting just like someone from the forties who wouldn't have liked rock and roll. On the other hand, maybe she was just upset that she couldn't join in!

Christy just stood there, looking very cool and collected. Every once in a while she'd pretend to type something on the computer. She really looked like a model in that skirt.

We were almost smack in the middle of the parade, so we kept having to stop when floats and marchers in front of us had to turn corners. Once when we were stopped, I saw Mr. Blaney in the crowd. "Hey, Mr. Blaney!" I called out, waving to him.

He grinned and gave me the thumbs-up sign with both hands.

Lots of people were taking pictures of us as we went by. I felt like a real celebrity!

"Psst," Stephanie hissed. I turned around. "Check out the right side of the float." She gestured with her head.

Taylor Sprouse was standing just a few yards ahead with his friends. He'd been calling Stephanie "Miss Spirit of Riverhurst" all week, and we hadn't bothered to tell him that we'd changed the float. I hoped he was surprised.

"I'm dying," Stephanie moaned, adjusting her headband.

"Relax, you look fine," I said out of the corner of my mouth. "At least you're not wearing go-go boots. Or a sheet."

She cracked up. Unfortunately, the band stopped playing just as we passed Taylor's group. I did *not* want to hear Taylor and his friends' comments — I had a feeling they wouldn't be flattering.

"Hey, look!" Taylor yelled. "Miss Spirit of Riverhurst. But she got a make-over! Like, wow, man, groovy! Far out!"

"Dig it, man!" one of his friends added. They all started laughing.

"And I was worried about a green sheet," Stephanie grumbled as our float rolled past him and turned the corner to head up to the high school. "He'd make fun of me no matter what I was wearing."

"Maybe you should start wearing all black," I suggested.

"Maybe I should just give up on Taylor Sprouse," she said gloomily.

"But what if that *Teen Topics* article is right, and he really, really, really likes you?" I asked.

"Lau-ren!" Stephanie said. "Give me a break!"

The parade ended at the "new" high school (it was still called new, even though it was about twenty-five years old). When we got closer I could see a big grandstand set up in front. An announcer was calling out the names of the floats, bands, and other marchers as they finished the parade.

"From Riverhurst Elementary, this float is called 'Riverhurst School Through the Years'!" the announcer said over the loudspeaker. "Look at those lovely young ladies! And, er, young gentlemen," he added, giving Henry — who was doing his best to act *just* like Elvis — a strange look.

A loud cheer came up from the stands. "This is great!" I said, turning back to smile at Christy.

But Christy wasn't smiling. In fact, she was definitely frowning. I went over to her. "Hey, Christy? What's the matter?"

"It's Ginger!" she said in a low voice. "She's over there." Christy looked kind of concerned. I knew how she felt. It's no fun to fight with your best friend — even if your best friend is Ginger Kinkaid!

I scanned the crowd outside the high school. I couldn't see Ginger at first, but then the float slowed down and suddenly I spotted her. She was standing on the edge of the crowd next to her mother. When Roger pulled to a stop — our part in the parade was over — we were almost face to face. Ginger was wearing a big coat and she had a scarf tied around her neck and face. I could see a few pockmarks on her cheeks, but she looked pretty healthy otherwise.

She also looked furious!

"She's pretty mad," Christy said.

"She's just upset that she couldn't be on such a great float," I said.

Kate came over to us. "What's going on?" she asked. "Why are you guys so huddled up?"

"Ginger's here," I said. "And she doesn't look happy."

"Don't worry," Kate said. "She'll get over it, eventually. I mean, it's not *your* fault she got the chicken pox," she told Christy.

Christy tried to smile. "No, I guess not," she mumbled.

Suddenly, a man carrying a notebook and a camera ran up to our float. "I love this float," he said. "It's the best one I've seen so far. I'd like to do a short write-up on it for the *Riverhurst Clarion,* if that's okay with you, of course."

"Sure," Kate grinned at me. "My first interview," she whispered. "Go ahead," she politely told the reporter.

"Who came up with the idea for this float? It's brilliant." The reporter stepped back and snapped a picture of the float.

I looked at Kate. How was she going to answer that question?

She cupped her hands around her mouth. "Ginger!" she called out. "Come over here!"

Ginger just glared at all of us.

"Come on!" Kate yelled.

Slowly, Ginger started walking over toward the float. "What?" she demanded when she got closer.

"I just wanted to tell this man who came up with the idea for our float," Kate said. "This is Ginger Kinkaid," she told the reporter. "He's from the *Clarion,*" she said to Ginger.

Ginger's eyes lit up and she moved even closer. She was still angry, but she was definitely interested.

"Ginger worked with us on the float but unfortunately she got sick and couldn't ride on it," Kate explained.

"It was Kate's idea, too," I put in. I didn't think Ginger should get all the credit.

"Actually, we all came up with different ideas for the float," Kate said. "Everyone contributed something."

The reporter made a few notes in his notebook. "That's terrific. Listen, I'd like to get a picture of all of you together!" he said.

"Not me," Ginger shook her head.

"Why not?" Kate asked.

"I look terrible," she muttered.

"No you don't," Christy said firmly. "Come up here and I'll fix your hair." She took a brush out of her pocketbook.

Ginger seemed reluctant at first, but then she got up on the float beside Christy. She took her scarf off and Christy quickly fluffed her hair around her face. When she was finished, Ginger looked fine.

"Is everybody ready?" the reporter asked us.

"Ready!" we all called back.

"Turn toward me!" he instructed us. "Move closer together."

We all put our arms around each other — even

Mark and Henry. I ended up standing between Patti and Mark.

"Okay, everybody," the reporter said, standing back and adjusting his camera lens. "Let's see some big smiles! Wait a minute. The two ringleaders should be in the middle. Ginger and Kate, move into the center, please," he instructed.

Kate looked at Ginger and shrugged. We all changed places so that they were standing in the middle.

"Now, put your arms around each other!" the reporter said cheerfully.

Kate slowly reached up and put her arm on Ginger's shoulder.

"Ready and . . . cheese!" the reporter shouted.

"Swiss!" Henry yelled as the camera snapped the picture.

Patti hit him on the arm. "You goofball!"

"Now, don't move for a minute. I'd like your names, so we can publish them underneath the photo." Kate named us in the order we were standing, and the reporter jotted them down.

After we told the reporter how we had come up with the props, who had lent us the clothes, and what classes we were in at school, he said he had enough information for his article. "Don't forget to buy the paper tomorrow!" he said. "I wouldn't be surprised if this makes the front page." Then he jogged back over to the grandstand to watch the rest of the floats and people in the parade.

Henry and Mark jumped down from the float. "I can't wait to get out of these clothes," Mark said, tugging at his Nehru collar.

"Neither can I," said Henry. "I mean, I like this leather jacket and everything, but it's really hot! And my hair feels like it's plastered to my head."

"I know the feeling," I said, laughing.

"See you later," Henry said. "It's been real!"

"Yeah — real groovy," Mark added. "Peace, man!" Then they took off for the high school.

A horn honked and a car pulled up beside us. "That's my mother," Ginger said. "I have to go home. Christy, do you want to come over for a little while?" she asked.

Christy beamed. "Sure!" she said. "Hey, see you guys later, okay? I had fun — thanks!"

"Wait, what about the stuff you left at my house?" Patti asked.

"I'll pick it up tomorrow," Christy said, stepping into the car.

"Wow, Ginger sure forgave her fast," Stephanie said after they drove off.

"Getting her picture in the paper probably helped," Patti commented. "She didn't seem too mad after that."

Kate hopped off the float and strolled around,

admiring it. "I'm going to buy *ten* copies of tomorrow's paper," she declared.

"Me too," I said. "I want to have a record of this historic day."

Patti grinned at me. "It's not every day that we march in a parade and get interviewed by the *Clarion*!"

"That's not what I'm talking about," I said, shaking my head. "I want a record of the day Kate Beekman put her arm around Ginger Kinkaid! Now that's what I call history!"

Sleepover Friends forever!

SLEEPOVER FRIENDS

#30 Big Sister Stephanie

Melissa folded her arms across her chest. "Stephanie invited me to her house. She's going to show me how to curl my hair."

"Sounds like a fun time," I muttered. Stephanie — playing Beauty Salon with *my* little sister?

"I can't wait!" Melissa declared. "I'm going to be so pretty, just like Stephanie."

What am I, chopped liver? I wanted to say. Now Melissa was not only dressing like Stephanie, she was also styling her hair the same way . . . what was next?

WIN A 10-SPEED BIKE!

Enter the
SLEEPOVER FRIENDS™
Ultimate Sleepover Giveaway!

Can you describe the ULTIMATE sleepover? Fill in the coupon below with your answers and you can win the ULTIMATE prize—a 10-Speed bike! Return by November 30, 1990.

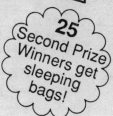

25 Second Prize Winners get sleeping bags!

Rules: Entries must be postmarked by November 30, 1990. Winners will be picked at random and notified by mail. No purchase necessary. Void where prohibited. Taxes on prizes are the responsibility of the winners and their immediate families. Employees of Scholastic Inc.; its agencies, affiliates, subsidiaries; and their immediate families not eligible. For a complete list of winners, send a self-addressed stamped envelope to Sleepover Friends Ultimate Sleepover Giveaway, Giveaway Winners List, at the address provided below.

Fill in the coupon below or write the information on a 3" x 5" piece of paper and mail to: SLEEPOVER FRIENDS ULTIMATE SLEEPOVER GIVEAWAY, Scholastic Inc., P.O. Box 754, 730 Broadway, New York, NY 10003. Canadian residents send entries to: Iris Ferguson, Scholastic Inc., 123 Newkirk Road, Richmond Hill, Ontario, Canada L4C365.

- -

Sleepover Friends Ultimate Sleepover Giveaway
Just fill in the blanks!

The ULTIMATE SLEEPOVER would be on a _____ night.
(pick a day)

We'd eat _____ , listen to _____ ,
(food)   (favorite music)

talk all night about _____ , watch
(fun topic)

_____ , and play_____ .
(movie/TV show)   (name of game)

Name _____ Age _____

Street _____

City_____ State _____ Zip _____

SLE290